MW01064482

The Redemption of Hiram Matthews
A Novel

Michael R. Parrish

Copyright © 2013 Michael R. Parrish

ISBN 978-1-62141-985-3

All rights reserved. No part of this publication may be reproduced, stored in a retrieval system, or transmitted in any form or by any means, electronic, mechanical, recording or otherwise, without the prior written permission of the author.

Published by BookLocker.com, Inc., Bradenton, Florida.

Printed in the United States of America.

The characters and events in this book are fictitious. Any similarity to real persons, living or dead, is coincidental and not intended by the author.

BookLocker.com, Inc.
2013

First Edition

ACKNOWLEDGEMENTS

For my wife, Suzanne, my best friend and love for forty seven years. Thanks for your encouragement and belief in me.

For Kimberly, my daughter, our first college graduate, wonderful mother, and successful business woman. Thanks for your example of success and hard work.

For Robert, my son, who has pursued and captured his own dream of becoming a pilot.

For Isabella, Gracie, Sammie and Bobby for believing that Grandpa can do anything.

Chapter One

Hiram Matthews knew what he had to do. He had thought about it all night. The decision had been in the making for some time, ever since the death of his beloved wife Sarah. Will Hardison's generous offer had made things much easier. As he lay staring at the ceiling of his small ranch house bedroom his resolve had strengthened. It didn't make any sense and he knew it, but he was finally at peace with the decision. He would speak to Aaron in the morning. He needed to know what was coming. He had been Hiram's foreman for almost eight years and during that time Aaron had come to be a true friend.

"Friends are hard to come by", he thought. "Good friends are even more rare. A man is lucky if he has two or three friends like Aaron during an entire lifetime. I hate to have to tell him."

The sun was beginning to peak in the east and Hiram had already lain in the bed later than he was accustomed. No sense in putting it off. Maybe he could catch Aaron before he and the hands rode out. He rolled out of the old four- poster that Sarah had loved.

"It's cold this morning," he thought. Cold seemed to bother him more and more with passing years. Too many falls, too many wild range steers, and too many nights spent sleeping on the ground. Building a ranch was tough work. It had been his passion before Ethan had disappeared. And then Sarah had died. That was the final blow. His passion was gone.

He slipped his trousers off the hook on the wall and slid into his well-worn boots. He walked to the porch and looked toward the bunk house. He saw the flicker of a lantern. He glanced toward the barn and Aaron was leading his saddled mount.

"Aaron, come on up to the house, I need to talk to you," he yelled.

"Be right there Hiram," Aaron replied. "Just let me make sure the boys are lined out."

"That's fine; I'll get some coffee on."

Hiram walked back into the kitchen and picked up the poker from the stand next to the stove and stirred the coals and ashes. He opened the door and threw in some kindling. A few strokes from the small bellows and the kindling took. "Damn" he thought to himself. It was hardest this time of day. Sarah was always the one to get the stove going and to put the coffee on. He missed her more than he could say. He had taken her death hard and he blamed himself. She had become deeply depressed when little Ethan had disappeared. Ethan loved playing in the small creek not more than two hundred yards from the house. He had wandered off while Sarah had been busy with chores. He was never seen again. It was clear that he had been abducted. Sarah blamed herself for his disappearance. "Why would they take our boy and not me?" she had asked a thousand times. Hiram was never able to reconcile that fact. Why? There was no answer.

He had tried everything that he could. He had turned more and more of managing the ranch over to Aaron so he could spend more time with Sarah. She had held on for seven years after Ethan's disappearance, but the last year had come crashing down on her. Her health had deteriorated over the years. The depression and the grief had taken their toll. And then the sickness had come. She had become too frail almost overnight to be able to move her to a city back east where she could receive any sort of medical help. There were no doctor's close by. There were home remedies and herbal concoctions. Nothing helped. There was no way to know what was wrong with her for sure. He just knew that she was wasting away and dying. Then in

June she has died. The end was rough and painful. It seemed as though all of her grief and sorrow had been transferred to him.

"How did I allow this to happen?" He had asked himself. "I should have sold this place years ago and taken her to St. Louis to be close to her family."

The ranch had killed her. Not so much the ranch itself. It was the constant reminder that her only child had been taken from her there. "If we had just gotten any idea of whether he was alive or dead, maybe she could have gotten some closure," he thought. It was the never knowing that had gnawed at the both of them for nearly seven years and now she was gone.

The knock on the door brought him back from his thoughts.

"Hiram, you wanted to talk to me?" Aaron called.

"Come on in Aaron."

Aaron Russell was tall and sinewy. His looks didn't tell his age. He had turned forty-five on his last birthday. Years of chasing cows had hardened and tanned his face to a well burnished bronze. He had wrangled cows since he was fourteen. It was pretty much all he knew. He could read and write a little, but the range had been his school and his life. The wrinkles around his eyes were from years of squinting at the Texas sun. A twinge of gray appeared on his temples. When his hat was off - which was bedtime, or meal time, or indoors - you could see that his hair was also beginning to thin. He wasn't an overly handsome man, but he certainly wasn't ugly either. His slightly bowed legs revealed that he had spent most of his life on horseback. He was a good wrangler and a better foreman. He always seemed to know what needed to be done and how it needed to be done. He was good with the hands. The men respected him and trusted him. He was the most honest man that Hiram had ever known.

"What's up Hiram?"

"Got something I need to tell you Aaron and it's not gonna be easy."

Aaron knew Hiram was straight spoken and would not dance around the matter whatever it was. He could tell it was something serious by the look on Hiram's face. "I hope I haven't done something," he thought. He took a seat at the kitchen table and waited.

"I've made a tough decision, Aaron. It hasn't come easy and it affects you and the boys. Best I say it straight out. Truth is I'm selling the ranch. Will Hardison is buying the place - lock, stock and barrel. He's a good man and honest. He'll keep you and the hands on."

Aaron sat for several moments as the news sunk in. "That's a cold wind out of the north. Why in the world would you want to do such a thing? I've known you - what - eight years, and I know how much of yourself you've put into building this place. I helped you bury Sarah right out there under the big oak. Why in the world would you want to give it all up? What are you planning on doin?"

Hiram set two cups on the table and poured coffee. "There's something I have to do Aaron and I can't have the worry of the ranch. I'm hell bent on finding my son."

Hiram and Aaron had talked about Ethan's disappearance. "My god, Hiram. I don't mean to be callus about it, but you have to know your boy is probably dead. We've talked about this. Indians don't normally keep male children. Hell, you don't even know for sure that's what happened to him. I know how much Sarah suffered with all this and now you want to go off looking for Ethan. Where? What direction? Where would you begin?"

"I know it don't make any sense Aaron. I just feel like I can somehow bring some peace to Sarah, even though she's gone. And this has been eating a hole in my gut too. I just don't believe the boy's dead. I never did. I know it in my bones that he's out there somewhere."

Aaron shook his head. "If you want my opinion, and I know before you say it, you didn't ask my opinion, but I believe what you're wanting to do is a damn fool thing. You've got the ranch, and the boys are a good bunch. We can keep this thing together for you if you need to be gone a while. If you sell the ranch there will be nothing to come back to. "

Hiram looked at Aaron with an "I know that you're right" look in his eye. "Aaron, you're more than just a ranch foreman to me. You're as good a friend as I've ever had. We think a lot alike, you and me. And in my heart I know you're probably right, but my mind's made up. My heart's not in the ranch anymore. You've been running the place since Sarah took sick. Besides, with what Will is paying me for the ranch and with what we got last summer when we sold most of the herd I'll never have to worry about money. It's just something I've got to do. If I don't do this, I might as well put a gun to my head."

Aaron looked at the floor for a long time. Neither man spoke. Neither needed to. Aaron stood and extended his hand. Hiram grasped his friend's weathered hand. The two men looked into one another's eyes and both simply nodded. Aaron looked at the floor again and then back into Hiram's eyes. "You want to tell the men or you want me to do it?"

"Best if I tell them personally. I owe them that much. I've got to go to Waco and I'll tell them when I get back. I'll leave at first light tomorrow. Probably be gone seven or eight days at least. If you can keep things going for a few days I'd appreciate it. "

"All right then," Aaron replied softly as he turned to leave.

Chapter Two

The ranch was only about six miles from Meridian, Texas. Meridian was a fledgling settlement of only about a dozen families. There were no stores or commerce. Waco was the nearest larger town with a bank and a lawyer. It had also been the site of a Ranger station.

When Ethan had disappeared, a young ranger corporal had been dispatched from Waco. It had taken days for word to summon help from the rangers, and longer still for the corporal to be dispatched. By the time he arrived the trail had grown cold and little indication was found of what had become of Ethan Matthews. Hiram hoped the ranger was still in Waco.

His concern right now was setting up the sale of the ranch. He knew he could trust Will to deposit the agreed funds for the purchase of the ranch into an account at the bank. All he needed was a lawyer to draw up the agreement and deliver it to the bank. And he knew exactly the lawyer he needed. It didn't matter that he was also probably the only lawyer in Waco. Zebediah Granger was an acquaintance and a man Hiram could trust. Granger had helped Hiram with the legal work when he had acquired his first few acres and cows and had written legal wills for both him and Sarah. Hiram just needed to get to Waco and back to the ranch as quickly as possible.

At first light the following morning he was up and saddling his horse. His bedroll, with a good slicker, clean pants and shirt rolled inside, was tied down and a few items he would need were tucked away in his saddle bags. Some jerky, salt pork, coffee, and a small pot were tucked in one bag and a small skillet and some necessities in the other. He liked having the skillet just in case he got lucky and was able to bag a swamp rabbit or cottontail for his supper. It would fry up pretty well with some of the salt pork. He was traveling light to make the best time he could. He checked his saddle straps and took a last look around the barn. He was ready. It would begin today.

Hiram placed a worn boot into a stirrup and swung into the saddle. "Good Lord," he murmured, "I've got to be crazy, so if you don't mind, I'm gonna need your help." He lightly kicked the horse's sides and set his sights to the east.

He had almost hoped that Aaron would be up to make another try to talk him out of his decision. But he knew that Aaron wasn't that sort of man. Once they had shook hands yesterday, it was done.

Bosque County, Texas was one of the most beautiful places Hiram had ever seen. That had made it easy to settle in the area. He had joined the army when he was no more than a teenager. He had hated it but he picked up some skills there. He had become an excellent marksman with both the pistol and rifle. He had been taught how to read signs by a Shoshoni scout. He had left the army with a small poke that he had saved from his wages and from pay-day poker games. He had moved on and worked as a wrangler and had held onto every dime of wages he could. He had always known he wanted to have his own place and nothing was going to keep him from it.

He knew that there was land for the taking in Texas. Under the Constitution of 1836 a single man could be given 320 acres of land. The only provision was that he fulfill his duty as a citizen and remain in the state for three years. When he thought he had enough saved to purchase a few good breeding cows and a good bull he had set out to find a place to make a beginning. When he rode into this area of Texas he knew this would be home.

He found a spot with good grass and water. There was a small box canyon and he was able to build sturdy fence across its entry. Come round-up time it had worked out well. Lawyer Zebediah

Granger helped him file the papers with the state to make it all legal. All Hiram had to do was to be able to hang on to the land.

There were wild Mexican longhorns and steers in the area and he was able to round up a good many early on, and had built a respectable herd in only a short time. It was hard work and he had fought weather, thieves, and every obstacle a man could imagine. He was beyond the line of the frontier and beyond the protection of the army. It had been pure dumb luck that he and his family had not been killed by renegade Indians or expatriated Mexicans. But he had persevered.

Early on he slept under the stars and brush arbors for far too many nights before he was able to build a small one room cabin. Within only a few years he was able to hire a hand or two and eventually he had built a livable cabin, bunk house, and barn.

 Much of the area where he had settled was mesquite and cedar thicket but there had been enough open areas to range cows. And the grass was really good. There were rolling hills and small canyons. There were good year- round creeks and the Bosque flowed through much of the area. Cacti and oak were plentiful as were mesquites and cedar. Deer and other game were also plentiful. Hiram hated to think that he might never return to this part of the state.

He had been riding about an hour when he spotted a small herd of deer, mostly does. He silently reigned in his big mare long enough to enjoy watching them. Hiram didn't like shooting deer. They were just too pretty to destroy. He had taken and eaten his share, but he never liked killing something that beautiful. But he would take that rabbit if he got a chance.

He was following a familiar creek picking his way through the brush. There was no well-defined trail he could follow so he would have to rely on memory and his navigating skill to make it to Waco. He had made the ride a number of times over the years and he had a good sense of direction. He could use the stars some and he knew approximately what easterly direction to take. He knew that the Bosque River was off to his left and if he kept his current direction he would strike the river sometime on the second day. It was a simple matter of following the Bosque until it met with the Brazos in Waco.

He rode through the day without event and had covered a fair distance. He had begun looking for a good spot to camp the night and was moving slowly along a small draw. His eye caught movement in the brush ahead. A small armadillo was busy turning over rocks and digging for his dinner. He had eaten armadillo, but not tonight. He pulled up in a small clearing close to the creek and slowly dismounted. "I've gotten soft," he thought to himself. "I feel like a horse kicked me in my back". He stretched and began untying his roll. After he had taken down his saddle and gear, he loosely hobbled his mare and let her begin feeding on the soft, tasty grasses. The air had grown noticeably cooler. It was going to be a cool night.

Once he had a good supply of wood gathered he settled down for the evening. "This ought to be different," he murmured to himself. "I haven't slept under the stars in a long time. I guess if it don't kill me I'll make it to Waco," he chuckled to himself. "Been on the trail one day and I'm complaining like an old woman already." A short while later he was sitting by a good fire with a cup of hot coffee in his hand. He realized something in him actually missed all this. "We'll see how I feel about that come morning," he said to himself.

Sleep came quickly for the first time in months. He didn't know how long he had been asleep when he sat bolt upright. The noise had awakened him and he felt like the hair on the back of his neck was standing straight up. It was a sound he had heard only twice before. He pulled on his boots and sprang to his feet. It was a big cat and it was close. He didn't know if the cat might be after his mare, but he wasn't taking any chances. He slipped his rifle from the saddle sheath and threw a shell into the chamber. He stuck his pistol under his belt. He could hear the big mare snorting and stomping. She was spooked too. His eyes adjusted to the dark as soon as he stepped away from the now glowing fire. He headed in the direction of the sounds from his mare.

"You're not having supper at my expense," he said. After only a few paces he could see the mare just a few steps across the small opening. She was continuing to paw the earth even though she was hobbled. He quickened his pace and in only a few steps he had his hand in the big mare's mane. His presence and low soothing voice had a calming effect on her.

"Whoa. It's OK girl," he said softly as he stroked her neck. "We're bigger and better armed." He began slowly moving the mare closer to the area by the fire. What happened next was surreal. The cougar sprang from the darkness on his right. In the dark the cat was nearly on them before his eye caught her. He whirled in the cat's direction as the big mare reared and jerked his hand from her mane. He managed to fire a wild shot in the cat's direction. The report from the rifle spooked the horse and she reared again. The shot had come nowhere close to finding its mark, but it had done the job. It was hard to tell who was the most scared, the horse, the cat, or Hiram. The big cat sprinted into the brush. Hiram fired a shot from his pistol in its direction just for good measure.

The big mare was still struggling against the hobble ropes. She was spooked and it was going to be tough to settle her down now. "Whoa. Whoa girl." Hiram began to try to get the big horse to hear his voice in an attempt to settle her down. She was all the way across the small clearing and Hiram spoke softly to the mare. "We'll be in a mess if you break a leg girl. I don't want to have to put you down and I sure as heck don't want to walk back home or to Waco. Whoa girl, whoa. Ain't no harm done yet, except to maybe my drawers." He continued to approach the mare and to speak softly to her. She was still pawing and snorting when he reached her side. "Whoa girl." He continued to sooth her with his voice. She was beginning to settle.

"By damn, this is some first night ain't it girl," he said to the big mare. "Guess it's a good thing we don't have polar bears here," he murmured jokingly. "What say you and I get a bit closer to a big fire for the rest of the night?" He knew sleep would be at a premium for the rest of this night. He would never be sure just exactly who the big cat had intended to eat!

The second morning broke cool and overcast. Hiram broke camp and stowed away his gear. "The only thing wrong with being alone on the trail is there's too much time to think," he said to the big mare. He had begun reflecting on another trip to Waco years ago. As he rode his mind went back in time. And his thoughts were of Sarah.

He had made a trip to Waco years before to buy supplies for the ranch. That was when he had met her. Hiram had zero experience when it came to matters of the heart. He'd not had the time. Female contact had been limited to an occasional visit to a whore house. He didn't much like that and his deviance had been few.

When Hiram entered the mercantile to purchase supplies for the ranch, Sarah was working behind the counter. As he stepped to the counter she turned to greet him. Her green eyes met his, and he was dumbstruck. She was taller than most women and thin. He could tell that her loose fitting dress hid a beautiful shape. Her auburn hair hung long down her back. Hiram was convinced in an instant that God had never created a lovelier creature.

"What can we do for you today?" She asked.

Her lips were full and her mouth turned up at the corners in a pleasant smile. Her teeth were straight and white.

"Well, I was just, um, uh, looking, uh, I need, uh...." His voice tapered off and he fell silent as he stared into her beautiful eyes.

"Cat got your tongue?" she asked.

"Oh, no. No. I just need to pick up some supplies." He fell silent again.

"I'll need a list, or you can just tell me what you need, and I can make a list." She stood silent waiting for Hiram to reply.

"Yes Ma'am," he said, "that would be good."

"Yes, you have a list, or yes, you want me to make one?"

"Oh yeah, I mean, yes Ma'am, I've got a list here somewhere," he said as he began to dig through his pockets. "You're new here aren't you? It's been a long while since I was here, but I don't recall seeing you before."

"I'm Sarah Hopkins." She stuck out her hand. "And yes, I am new to Waco."

"Your family here?" he asked as he shook her hand.

"Actually," she said, "I came here to visit my uncle. My parents are back in St. Louis. There wasn't a lot to hold me there, so when Uncle Jim, my Mother's brother, wrote complaining that he couldn't find any decent help here for the store, I decided to come out and work for him. I thought I might see a bit of Texas, but this is as far as I've gotten. How about you?"

"How about me?" He asked. "Oh, you mean do I live here? I have a small spread about three days ride northwest from here. Excuse my manners, I'm Hiram Matthews." He stuck out his hand and they shook. Her hand was warm and small in his. "I couldn't speak three minutes ago," he thought "and I'd tell her my life story now if she asked." He was right. Her easy, friendly manner and smile had set him at ease.

"Pleased to meet you Mr. Matthews," she replied. She examined his face with her green eyes. "A little rough around the edges," she thought. But she liked what she saw. His face was beginning to wrinkle a bit from the days spent in the relentless Texas summer sun. His skin was weathered and brown. His hair was full and a rusty brown color. So many men of the day wore a mustache. Not Hiram. "Not like so many of the men here in town that I've met," she said to herself. When they had shook she had noted that his hands were calloused and hard. There wasn't an ounce of fat on him. His shoulders were square and muscled and his six foot frame looked to be strong. He wasn't a bad looking man. He was obviously a man well acquainted with hard work. He had been three days on the trail and needed a bath and a shave. "I bet he cleans up pretty well," she mused.

"I'll start rounding up the things I can lift," she said. "You may need to help me with the bags of flour and beans."

They had exchanged a few more pleasantries as they worked to get his supplies together and loaded. When they were through she stuck out her hand again.

"Pleasure to make your acquaintance," she said.

"Nice to meet you," he replied.

"I guess that's it then." She smiled.

"I'll just be on my way then," he said as he walked toward the door. "Ask her, ask her – he was telling himself. Find some backbone." He stopped and turned. Summoning every ounce of fortitude he had he called her name.

"Uh, Ms. Hopkins, uh, look, I'm not very good at this sort of thing, and I know I must look pretty rough right now, and I hope I'm not being too forward - I'm not headed out till in the morning. I've got to eat supper, and I was hoping that maybe you would like to eat." He stammered. "I mean - with me. That is if you aren't seeing someone, or if you don't have plans, or..."

"Stop talking Hiram," she interrupted. She had called him by his given name. "I'd be delighted to join you for dinner. There is a nice little place just down the street. There's a sign in the window. The name is "Lydia's". Will seven be all right?"

"I believe seven will work just fine," he replied. "Should I call on you here at the store or your Uncle's house?"

"I'll meet you at Lydia's," she replied.

When he turned to leave the store he had a huge smile on his face.

They had taken dinner together. She had talked about her parents and family. Hiram didn't talk a lot. He was enjoying just looking at her beautiful face and hearing her talk. But they had hit it off. He was as comfortable with her as he'd ever been with anyone.

And that was how it had begun. Hiram had made two more trips to Waco before he had gotten the courage to ask Sarah to be his wife. He had been in love with her since the first moment he had laid eyes on her.

As he rode deep in reflection, he was recalling every word that she had spoken on that first meeting. He could almost feel her presence. CRASH!! A clap of thunder nearly caused him to jump from his saddle. "Good Lord," he yelled aloud as he was jerked from his reflections. "What in the world? Thunder in February? I hope that isn't some sort of omen," he said to the big mare. He rode the remainder of the day in a drizzling rain.

He arrived in Waco on the third evening without further incidence. He was anxious to speak to Zebediah and Samuel Walker, but he knew that would have to wait. He hadn't been in Waco in a long while. He needed to find a stable for his mare and a place to bunk the night. He'd get his business done tomorrow.

Chapter Three

He awoke just before dawn, the same as he had done nearly every day for the past twenty years. He had found a suitable stable for his mare and had slept with her in the stall. There was a barbershop with a bathhouse. He had gotten a bath and shave and dressed in the clean pants and shirt.

"Not going into a bank smelling and looking like some tramp trail hand," he had thought.

It was obvious that Waco had grown from a settlement along the Brazos River to a bustling town. The Huaco Indians had established a large community in the same area long before white men had come, and there was still a very small community of the Huaco culture in the area. But the bulk of Waco's white culture and business was laid out along several streets beginning at the river and running southwest.

The air was cool and clear and Hiram decided to walk the short distance to the bank. He wondered if Sarah's Uncle was still alive, much less still operating the goods store. He had been somewhat elderly when Hiram had first met Sarah. Over the years they had lost contact. He remembered fondly again the little restaurant where he and Sarah had dined. As he walked he kept a watchful eye out for either.

There was a small cafe at about the same location where he estimated Lydia's had been, but there was no name in the window, only a small sign hung outside the door that simply said "Cafe". He looked toward the sun and estimated the time to be around eight o'clock. "Might as well have a cup of coffee," he said aloud. He entered and looked around. There were several small tables set with calico covers. An attractive woman, probably in her thirties, was busily serving the only other customers in the place. Hiram took a seat and waited. After only a few moments the woman approached his table.

"Good morning," she said. "What can I get for you, cowboy?"

"Just a black coffee, please Ma'am." In a moment she was back with a pot of coffee and a cup. "You from around these parts?" she asked as she poured his coffee.

"Just in town to take care of some business."

"Sure you won't have some breakfast?" she asked. Julia Smith liked to cook and she liked to feed hungry people, especially cowboys. Hiram shook his head as he swallowed a bit of coffee. "No thank you," he said. I really do need to move along."

"Suit yourself, but I make the best biscuits and gravy in this part of Texas." She was bragging, but she was right. Her place was normally packed, but many of her regulars had come and gone.

"I was wondering if I could ask you a question." Hiram said.

"Shoot."

"Some years ago I dined with my wife at a small cafe here. That was when Waco was nothing more than a settlement. The place was called "Lydia's". I have fond memories of the occasion. I was wondering what might have become of it."

"Well now, this is your lucky day, cowboy," she said. "Lydia was my Mother. She passed away a number of years ago. The old place would have been just down the street a way. After her death I tried a few things, but cooking was what I knew best. Mom taught me, and she was a good cook. So, I borrowed a few dollars from Mr. Scoggins down at the Texas Bank and opened up this little place."

"Well I'll be darned," he said. "And I am sorry to hear about your Mother."

She stuck out her hand. "I'm Julia Smith. Pleased to meet you Mr....?"

"Hiram, Hiram Matthews," he answered as he shook her hand. "You mentioned the Texas Bank and a Mr. Scoggins? It so happens that's where I'm headed."

"Yep. Elvin Scoggins is the banker. He's a little squint of a man, but he's nice enough, and honest," she said. "He runs the bank and Mrs. Larksford tellers for him. The bank's down to the corner and left. They should be open by now."

"Then I need to be on my way." he said. "I've other business than the bank. It's nice to make your acquaintance."

"Hope you'll come back for supper if you're still here."

They shook hands and he set out to speak with Mr. Scoggins.

The bank was a small building tucked away on the side street. There was a small sign in the window that said "open". Hiram entered and looked around. Across the single room there was a teller window and a small railed area. A small man sat behind a desk and was busily studying some documents. He did not acknowledge Hiram's presence.

The man was bald on the top of his head with a band of hair encircling the sides. He was portly and round. He wore spectacles which were perched on the tip of his nose. His eye brows were bushy and dark and his large mutton chop sideburns extended well down his fat cheeks. He was dressed in a suit appropriate for a man of stature. From Alice's description Hiram assumed he was the banker, Mr. Scoggins. He walked to the rail and waited. The man still did not look up from his work.

"Excuse me sir," he said, perhaps a bit louder than needed.

The little man lowered the paper he was examining and looked over the top. He squinted as he looked in Hiram's direction. "Julia was right," Hiram thought. "He is a squint."

The banker examined Hiram for a moment as if he were unsure who had spoken. After a moment he spoke. "Can I help you, sir?" His voice was a bit squeaky and raspy all in one, and Hiram thought how he sounded like an overgrown mouse.

"I need to speak to someone concerning a transaction," he said.

"Mrs. Larksford will be right out and she can help you," the banker said summarily.

"I believe my business may require more than the help of a teller," he said, pretending not to know with whom he was speaking.

Mr. Scoggins lowered the papers again. He studied Hiram for a moment then pushed back from his desk. "Then I believe you will require my services," he said as he stood. "Come on over and let's see if we can help you." He gestured with open hand to the straight back chair next to the desk. "I'm Elvin Scoggins," he said as he extended his hand.

"And I'm Hiram Matthews," Hiram replied as his grasped the banker's hand.

"Now, what can we do for you?"

The little man listened as Hiram explained that he was selling his place and needed to open an account for deposit of funds. He explained that Mr. Granger, his lawyer, would deliver papers for the transaction covering the sale of his place and that a Mr. Will Hardison would presently come to Waco to sign all documents and deposit funds to cover the deal. He added that he may need to draft against the account from time to time from other locations and inquired if that were possible. After Hiram had given full explanation of his wishes Mr. Scoggins leaned back in his chair.

"I can't imagine why a man your age would be selling out, but I suppose that would be none of my concern and I suspect that you have your reasons," he said as he searched Hiram's face as though he were expecting that more information was forthcoming.

"I have," was the only reply.

"Well then, I'll be expecting to hear from Zebediah presently. Mrs. Larksford will help you with the account."

After introductions, the papers were completed. He thanked Mrs. Larksford and Mr. Scoggins and set out to find Zebediah.

Chapter Four

Zebediah Granger had grown up in the east. His mother was a school teacher in the town where he was raised. His father had worked as a clerk in a bank and had been tragically killed in a botched robbery attempt at the bank when Zeb was a young boy. The man who shot his father was a half-witted drunk. He was near penniless and while in a drunken stupor had hatched the idea that he should rob the bank. He had gotten hold of an old pistol. He had entered the bank and fired a shot into the air. The bullet had struck a metal plate in a beam and ricocheted striking his father in the head. He was killed instantly. Dead by the reckless act of a witless drunk.

Zeb's mother had remained in the town and had raised Zeb on her own. He was small and scholarly as a boy and learned an appreciation of books and learning from his mother. She had been able to see to it that Zeb received as good an education as she could afford him under her tutelage. His father's tragic death had made him angry and withdrawn during his younger years.

When Zeb had reached sixteen his mother had arranged for Zeb to go to work for a friend in his law office. Zeb had proven to be an apt pupil and showed a real interest in the law. He had studied hard and was a voracious reader. He had consumed every law book and work that he could find concerning the law. Zeb had found his calling. He had become an excellent assistant in the law office. He had come out of his shell and was developing into a fine young man, and he had obtained a good understanding of the law.

In the year he turned twenty his mother had taken ill and died. After his mother's death he had become despondent for a time and had grown restless. He had no desire to attend law school. After hearing stories of Texas, he had made the bold decision to go west.

He had eventually worked his way to Texas and had settled in what was to become Waco. There had been nothing more there than a trading post that had been established on the banks of the Brazos River. He had endeared himself to the owner, Mr. George Barnard and worked at the trading post for several years.

Texas had not yet become a state, and under Republic law he had been granted head-rights to 320 acres of land. He soon realized that he had no affinity for the land. He realized that Texas needed practitioners of the law. Although he had never graduated from any school with a degree, he soon found that he could practice law by simply hanging out a shingle. He had done so, and as settlers moved into the region he had established himself as a lawyer and had stayed in Waco.

Waco was now becoming a fledgling town of importance in Texas, and he had become a respected business man and lawyer.

He sat at his desk working and looked up when he heard Hiram enter. He had last seen Hiram years ago when he had drawn up wills for him and Sarah, but he recognized Hiram almost immediately.

"By god," he said as he rose from his desk. "I never forget a face and I believe your's belongs to Hiram Matthews. The years have been good to you. (It was a statement he would soon regret having said.) I'd have recognized you anywhere." Zeb approached and extended a hand. "Of all the people I was expecting to walk into my office today, I can assure you that it would not have been you. It's been maybe eight or ten years since I last saw you. I believe I wrote wills for you and your wife on that occasion."

Hiram was amazed at the man's ability to remember names and faces. He had a mind like a steel trap and the years had not diminished his ability. Nor had it diminished his size. At six-one and two hundred pounds he was a formidable man. His silver hair was long and combed straight back to cover the balding crown of his head. Although he would have been a good catch for any woman, he had remained single.

"I expect that would be about right," Hiram said. "How are you Zeb?"

"I am doing well, and seeing an old acquaintance always makes me feel better," he offered.

Zeb was in fact doing very well. He had his law practice and owned several small businesses in Waco. He was a well-respected man and there had been talk of a making him a judge. Before the war some were even talking of making him a senator.

The war was changing everything in Texas. So many people and resources were being funneled into the war effort, and that had opened up challenges and opportunities. Movement of goods and supplies had become a good business avenue for Zeb. Troop strength along the frontier had been diminished. The Confederacy had taken over all federal forts along the frontier. But Indian activity and raids were increasing. Bands of white brigands and gun runners had also increased. Law and order had become harder to maintain, and the citizens had seen Zeb as a real possibility to help in the effort. But Zeb had no real interest in entering politics in any way. He had too many business interests that were working well for him.

"I remember that you settled a place west of here on the fringe of the settled frontier. I believe I helped you with your head-right allotment," he added. "It was a bold thing you did. I'm surprised that you and your wife didn't get your scalps lifted. And speaking of wives, how is your wife? Is she with you?"

"I lost Sarah last June," Hiram said sadly.

"By god, I am sorry to hear that Hiram. I remember she was a comely woman and friendly. I recall she was from this area. Sorry to hear of your loss."

"Zeb, I've a favor to ask of you," Hiram blurted, not wishing to be drawn into any more of the story than needful. "I need you to help me with the sale of my place."

"You're selling your ranch?" he asked incredulous. "Why in the world are you doing that? Does it have to do with the death of your wife?"

"In part it does, Zeb. There is something that I have to do and I may need part of the money from the sell." With that he went into the story of Ethan's disappearance and his plan to find his son.

Zeb sat silent at the end of the account. He regretted his remark about the years being good to Hiram. He stood and walked around his desk and sat on the edge.

"Hiram," he said, "I want to talk straight here. I admire your pluck. I do. But you have to know in your heart that you have a snowball's chance. The Comanches have taken and sold children up and down the frontier for years. They could have sold your boy anywhere from here to Mexico, if they didn't kill him. I know my language may seem harsh, but I believe that what you are doing is a mistake. It seems hasty and ill advised to me. Not to mention that you will probably get your cajones cut off by some band of Indians. Raids along and west of the frontier have increased since the war began. There's little help out there anymore. You get into trouble and you'll get yourself killed."

"That seems to be a popular opinion," Hiram replied. "My ranch foreman said the same thing, but I am bound to see this through."

Zeb sat silent for a few moments. "I'm probably helping you get yourself killed, but if this is what you want, I'll handle it for you. I'll begin work on it today and will have everything ready for you to sign sometime tomorrow afternoon. Where are you staying and what are you doing about supper?"

Hiram told him he had slept in the stable the night before.

"No, no. That won't do for tonight. There is a small hotel down the street. It's reasonable and clean. Let the man at the stable know you will leave your horse there tonight, but you will be seeking other accommodations for yourself."

Hiram nodded. "I had coffee at a nice cafe a bit ago, and the owner insisted that I come back for supper. I believe her name is Julia Smith."

"I know the cafe. Julia serves the best biscuits and gravy in this part of the state," Zeb replied. "But tonight feels like a steak and potatoes night. My treat. Let's get you set for the night at the hotel and I'll come back around at about six. We can walk to the establishment. It'll do me good."

Chapter Five

The place where Zeb took Hiram was more a saloon than a restaurant. But they served meals and had the best steak in town. Zeb liked the place. He could get a fine steak and enjoy a nice sip of whiskey after his meals. The place could get a bit rowdy from time to time but there was seldom any real trouble. The town sheriff did a good job controlling rowdies.

The two men had enjoyed small talk as they ate and sat visiting following the meal. Three men sat at the table behind them. They had more the look of buffalo hunters than town folk. They had been drinking whiskey and had consumed more than their share. As they had continued to drink they had become louder and several customers had hastily finished their meals or drinks and left. Hiram was bothered by their coarseness, but he figured they were of no concern to him. They were just an annoyance.

"So what's your plan, Hiram?" Zeb asked. "Where in the devil will you start?"

"After we finish our business at the bank tomorrow I thought I'd go over to Fort Fisher to see if Sam Walker is still there. I assume there are still troops there and am hoping the rangers have some men there."

"No. No, Hiram. The rangers gave up on Fort Fisher a number of years ago. I would have thought you knew that. I believe Sam Walker is now at Fort Graham up toward Ft. Worth. There are rangers in and out of Waco, but none are stationed here. Since the secession the rangers are pretty dysfunctional. There's lots of politics involved and no one seems to know whether the rangers will even be official. Most of the Huacos were moved to reservations in Indian Territory back in fifty-nine.

Hasn't been much reason for rangers to be stationed here since then. But I'll check to see if any happen to be in town."

The scruffy men at the next table were quieter and growing more sullen as they continued to order more drink. Hiram and Zeb were unaware that the men were listening to their conversation.

"Damned Rangers, if you ask me," one of the men muttered. He appeared to be the worst of the bunch. He was unkempt, as were the others, and had a large scar across the right side of his face. His eyes were deep set and menacing. He had begun to stare at Zeb and Hiram. "We need another round over here," he shouted at the barman.

A man appeared at the swinging doors that led to the kitchen area to see what was going on. He approached the men at the other table.

"Perhaps you men would be more comfortable finishing your evening elsewhere. I believe you've had enough to drink," he announced.

"He's got lots of nerve. Either that or he's just plain crazy," Hiram thought as he watched the scene unfold.

"We like it fine right here in your little place. You just keep the whiskey coming and mind your mouth lest I give you the back side of my hand," the burly man growled and tapped the table with the tip of his finger. The owner's courage seemed to falter a bit as the ruffian glared at him.

"Just keep it down," he said as he hurriedly exited to the rear of the establishment.

"Keep you down, you little turd," the man retorted. They all laughed.

Hiram and Zeb resumed their conversation.

"I had hoped to find Walker here. He was the ranger sent out when Ethan disappeared. I hoped that maybe there was something he could tell me. Maybe something he missed. I don't know."

Zeb took a sip of the whiskey he had ordered.

"Well, the war has affected everything Hiram. I told you earlier that Indian activity has increased since the war began. The army hasn't the man power to properly guard the frontier. Things had gotten better until the war and now things are going to hell. What rangers are left stay on the move pretty much. They're spread thin."

"We've been isolated at the ranch," Hiram replied. "I'm afraid I don't know or understand much about this war."

"It's a damn mess is what it is, Hiram. The accepted belief is that it's about slavery. Folks up north under the Union flag want slavery abolished. Folks under the Confederacy want to keep their slaves to plant and harvest their crops and such. So what it's really about is money. The south may not survive without slaves to work the field and do the labor required to get goods to market." He shook his head. "There's gonna be a lot of men die in this war."

"I don't hold with the idea that one man can own another," Hiram stated his belief. "The whole idea of slavery seems cruel and barbaric to me. Seems foolish for men to die in such a dispute."

Hiram had put the men at the other table out of his mind when he and Zeb had started talking. The mean looking one stood suddenly and his chair went clattering across the floor. He spun in Hiram's direction and glared.

"You some kinda Blue Belly nigger lover?" he blurted.

Hiram was unaware that the man had heard his conversation with Zeb. The man's sudden, fierce outburst took him by surprise and he sat looking at the man but didn't speak.

"I'm speaking to you, mister. You some kind of nigger lover, are ya?"

Hiram tried to keep his composure. His gut told him to be careful in how he handled the situation. The man was obviously drunk, and Hiram didn't savor the idea of a fight. "Don't let this bully get to you," he thought.

"I'm just having a quiet meal and conversation with my friend here." Hiram remained seated and began to assess what to do if the man continued to press him. The table had not been cleared and a steak knife still lay on his plate. If the man was armed in any way, the knife would be handy. He turned his attention back to Zeb hoping that if he pretended to ignore the man that maybe he would cool off. His disdain had the opposite effect.

"We got us a dumb, cowboy, nigger lover here boys," the man snarled. The other men laughed.

"Look friend," Hiram replied, "we're not looking for any trouble here."

The man took a step closer to Hiram and Zeb. "I ain't your friend, nigger lover. And you got trouble! I got a mind to give you the beatin' you deserve, nigger lover."

"I don't much care for that term friend. It doesn't mix well with a man's supper. Let's just say that you and I see things differently and leave it at that." Hiram said as he stood. He was beginning to sense that talking the man down was a lost cause.

"I told you, you dumb cowboy, I ain't your friend."

"My mistake. Sorry if I offended you. No need for you and me to come to blows." Hiram chose his words carefully, but his insides were beginning to boil.

The man's anger was growing.

"Blows?" he blurted. "I'm gonna beat the hell out of you, you damn nigger lover."

Hiram sensed that things were about to go badly and he felt himself beginning to tense even more. The man had closed the gap between himself and Hiram and stood at no more than arm's length away. He was mean looking and slightly bigger than

Hiram and he realized that he could not let the man get the upper hand. He was prepared to do whatever it took if it came to a fight. He still did not speak. This infuriated the man and he suddenly drew back a fisted hand to strike. Before he could uncoil, Hiram threw up his left arm and unleashed a hard right hand. It caught his opponent flush in the nose. Hiram felt the crunch of breaking cartilage. The bully staggered backwards. Hiram shifted his weight and brought a hard left uppercut to the man's jaw. The man reeled, his eyes blurred with splattered blood. Hiram grabbed a heavy ceramic coffee cup from the table and brought it down hard to the side of the man's head. The bully sank to his knees at the edge of the table. Hiram grabbed a hand full of hair. He jerked the man's head back and brought it down hard against the table edge. The bully crumpled to the floor.

Zeb was watching everything take place. The other men had gotten out of their chairs. Zeb reached inside his jacket and withdrew a small pistol.

"Better that we let this be between my friend and yours," he said. "This little pistol may not kill you but it will take off a knee cap, and I hit what I shoot at." He lied. He had never actually fired the gun, but he was willing to shoot; maybe even shoot to kill if it came to that.

Hiram stood with clenched fists waiting to see if the man was down to stay. He was still seeing red and his heart was pumping wildly. The man did not move.

"I think we'll be leaving now," Zeb announced to the other men. He reached out and took Hiram by the arm.

"The town sheriff is a friend of mine, and he will be coming shortly to look for you three. I suggest you scrape up your friend here and get out of town." He kept the gun pointed at the two as he and Hiram headed to the door. When they were out into the street he let go of Hiram's arm.

"By god," he exclaimed. "That bully never laid a hand on you. It don't pay to push you too far." Hiram did not speak.

"You OK my friend?" Zeb patted Hiram's arm.

"I'm fine," he replied. "I'm sorry I got you into that mess." Hiram's fury was subsiding.

"Wasn't your doing, Hiram," Zeb assured him. "I probably shouldn't have brought you to this place. Probably should have taken you up on the biscuits and gravy. That buffalo hunter was looking for trouble and he was drunk. He got what he deserved. I can't abide his drunken kind." He thought of his father.

"It's a good thing he was drunk. It slowed him down. It could have gone differently if he hadn't been. He'd likely have beat the tar out of me. Would you have shot those other two?" he asked.

"As sure as I'm standing here," Zeb replied. "I think we better get you back to the hotel and off the street before they gather themselves and come looking for us. I'll notify the sheriff to look them up and run 'em out of town. I'll square up with the owner later."

Hiram Matthews was not through with Keven Mallory and his cousins. Their paths would cross again.

Chapter Six

Hiram dropped by the cafe for breakfast, and inquired and found that Sarah's uncle had passed away. Zeb finished the papers the next afternoon as he had promised. He had spoken to the sheriff concerning the previous evening's events. Deputies had been sent to find the men from the saloon. They had disappeared.

Hiram and Zeb stood on the wooden walkway outside the bank.

Hiram extended his hand. "I guess that's it then Zeb. I want to thank you for your help over the years. You have been kind and I appreciate your friendship. I hope that I'll see you again my friend."

"Hiram, I wish there were some way that I could talk you out of this whole darned notion." There was genuine sadness in his face. He did like Hiram, and he admired him. "But I believe that you won't be swayed. So, there is something I want to ask of you. I doubt a company of rangers can do what it is that you are trying, much less a man alone. You need help. I've done some inquiring and there is an Indian fellow living just up river here. He has been a scout, I am told. His name is Two Colors. He speaks English. I am told he is reliable and does not care for Comanches. I am told he can be depended on. I want you to see if he can be hired, and I want you to take him with you."

"Zeb, I appreciate what you are trying to do. But you said it yourself. This is probably a fool's errand. I can't drag someone else into my troubles. I don't know what may befall me and I want no one else on my conscience. I don't know the man. I don't want to put my trust in a complete stranger."

"Just think about it. Maybe just talk to the man," Zeb pleaded.

"If it will make you feel better, I will think on it. How would I find him?"

Zeb supplied Hiram with directions. The two men stood for a silent moment.

Zeb spoke again. "If by some divine providence you find your boy and you need to make a new start, you come back here to see me. I'll help you make it happen."

"Then I guess it's good bye, my good friend," Hiram said.

"I hope you find your son, Hiram. God speed you on your journey."

Zeb stood watching as Hiram rode away. "You come back, my friend," he whispered.

Chapter Seven

Hiram set his direction for the ranch. He was hoping to make a few miles before sundown. But he had been thinking about what Zeb had said. "It would be good to have someone who had better tracking skills. Better still to have someone who can communicate with Indians," he had thought. "No harm in talking," he said to his mare as he patted her neck. He reined his mare toward the confluence of the Brazos and Bosque Rivers.

Two Colors was of mixed race. His mother was a Huaco Indian. His father was a white buffalo hunter. He had met Two Colors' mother in the Huaco settlement near Waco. Huaco women were often some of the prettiest among the various Indian cultures and were sought after as wives. His father had traded for Two Color's mother and had taken her as a wife according to Huaco tradition. He had taken her with him on his hunts. After a couple of years, following the birth of Two Colors, he had grown tired of her and abandoned her. She was left on the plains with a baby, a dog, and only a few days food and water.

His father had simply ridden away and was never heard from again. She had somehow survived and had walked back to Waco and the few Huacos that had remained there. Two Colors and his mother had remained with kin in the Huaco settlement and she had raised him there on the banks of the Brazos. When the Huacos were herded onto reservations, Two Colors had managed to find a place in the army as a scout. After a time he had come back to his current place near Waco. The citizens of Waco saw him as no threat and he was tolerated by the community. He now lived in a grass hut about a half mile north of where the two rivers joined.

It took Hiram some hunting to find the hut. He had thought about what he might say to the man. "Hello, my name is

Matthews, and I've come to see if you want to wander around with me and probably get yourself killed? Or maybe "My name is Matthews and I was just wondering if you could help me find someone that I don't even know is still alive," he said sarcastically to himself. "Maybe I am crazy," he thought.

He spied the hut about where Zeb had said he would find it. It looked like the bottom half of a giant hour glass. He felt he should approach with caution. He didn't want to get himself shot before he could even get well out of Waco. He reigned in his mare about one hundred feet from the hut. He sat and watched to see if anyone were stirring. Smoke drifted slowly from the center of the hut. No movement.

He rode closer. "Hello," he yelled and waited. Still no movement. "Hello," he called again. Then off to his left he heard the "click, clack" of the bolt being thrown on a rifle.

"Who are you and what do you want?" The voice came from the same direction.

"I'm looking for a man called Two Colors."

"You the law?" came the reply.

"My name is Hiram Matthews and I need to speak with Mr. Colors." He winced.

"Mr. Colors? You some kind of smart ass, white man?"

"I need to talk with the man, that's all."

"Climb down from that mare and walk to the opening by the hut. And keep your hands where I can see them," came the reply.

A man appeared from the brush to Hiram's left. He was holding a rifle and it was aimed squarely at Hiram.

"Are you Two Colors?" Hiram asked as the man continued to approach.

"I've been called by that name some. I go by another name now. If you're not the law, why you out here?"

Hiram thought a second before he replied. "I have need of someone who can track and speak Indian."

"Well, I can track, but I can't speak Indian. I don't know what that is. I speak English, Comanche, and Wichita. I can cuss in Spanish," he replied.

"I'm in need of a good man and can pay forty dollars a month, Mr.......?"

"Name's Joshua. Don't ever call me Two Colors. And I ain't looking for a job," he said flatly.

"You haven't heard me out. Can you put the gun down and let me explain?"

"I don't trust no white man that ain't ranger or army. You ain't either."

Hiram was beginning to wonder why he was wasting his time. "You're right. I'm neither. I'm a father who wants to find his son and I need help with that. It's that simple, but if you aren't interested, you aren't interested. I'll be on my way."

"What happened to your son? He lost?"

"No, my son is not lost. He was taken by raiders, probably Comanche."

"And you want me to track the bunch that took him?" Joshua asked. "I don't like Comanches," he added.

"I suppose you could say that."

"You drink coffee, white man?"

Hiram nodded. Joshua lowered the gun and motioned toward the large hut. "Come on in and let's talk."

The inside of the hut was lined with skins and there was a sturdy cot. There was a fire ring in the middle of the hut and a small fire was burning. There were skins scattered around the fire ring. The cot, a small table, and a large wooden box were the only furniture. Joshua went to the box and pulled out a small sack of coffee and two tin cups. The pot sat next to the fire ring. Once the coffee was hanging over the fire he turned his attention to Hiram, who had sat on a skin by the fire.

"You said you thought Comanche took your son."

"I can't be absolutely certain, but nothing else seems to make much sense," Hiram replied.

"If it's true, I would think you ain't too fond of Indians. And you want me, an Indian, to help you find him?" Joshua offered.

"I bear the Comanche nor any other man malice. I just want to find my son."

Joshua thought about Hiram's words for a moment.

"Your boy. How old?" he asked abruptly.

"He would be about twelve now."

"How many days since he was taken?"

"Well," said Hiram "It's been a number of days."

"So, how many is a number? Two, three?"

"The boy was taken about seven years ago." Hiram said flatly.

Joshua laughed and stared intently at Hiram. "I'm a good tracker, mister, but I don't do miracles."

"I don't need you for tracking as much as I need you to translate and scout." Hiram explained. "I'm headed back to my place, and then I'm going north to Ft. Graham. I hope to get an idea of where to look from a ranger up there and I could use your help."

"You got a name white man?"

"I'm Hiram Matthews," he said as he extended his hand.

"You're crazy Matthews? Your boy's probably dead," Joshua exclaimed.

"Next man tells me that, I'm gonna shoot." Hiram said grimly.

Joshua raised a hand with his index finger pointing at the sky. "But - I got a soft spot for crazy fathers lookin' for their lost sons. But doin' crazy will cost you fifty dollars a month."

"Done," Hiram replied. He liked the straightforward nature of the man. "Gather what you need for the trail. We can still make a few miles before nightfall."

"Too late in the day, Matthews. Get your bedroll, and you can sleep in here tonight. We can leave at first light. Besides, the coffees done," he said as he pointed at the pot.

Chapter Eight

Kwashnai Nocona sat by the fire warming his hands. Shining Rocks sat next to him. Nocona turned to Shining Rocks and spoke.

"In two days we will seek the white man Mallory to trade for guns and bullets. Then we will kill whites. They foul our lands with their smell and their farms. Every season they take more of the land that has belonged to our fathers and their fathers. They killed our fathers and elders at the Council House. When they attacked us at the Pease River only a few of us escaped. They killed Peta Nocona. They have no honor and we can never trust their promises. It has been many seasons, and I have not forgotten. Buffalo Hump made the white man pay, and now we will make them pay for their treachery. We will no longer just take their cattle and horses. We will rape their women and cut off their children' ears and noses and boil them in hides. We will not become old and give up like Buffalo Hump."

Shining Rocks nodded in agreement.

The Council House affair was historically called a fight. In fact, it had been a senseless slaughter of virtually unarmed Comanche elders, women, and children. After years of war with the whites the Comanches had sued for peace. A meeting was arranged at the Council House in San Antonio. The Texans had demanded that all captives be released as a provision of discussing peace terms. What they failed to understand was that the Comanche people were not a united nation like Mexico or the United States. The Comanches who were to be at Council House only spoke for portions of the entire Comanche people. When they were able to bring only one or two captives to the meeting the whites were enraged and saw it as a betrayal of the spirit of the negotiations. Chief Muguara had tried to explain that captives were being held throughout the camps of the entire Comanche people and that he could not demand of them that they also release their captives. The whites simply believed that the Comanche were trying to hold onto captives to negotiate for goods and money for their release. At some point during the talks the Comanche leaders were informed that they would be held in the jail until all of the captives were delivered. The Comanche leaders, armed only with knives, decided to try to fight their way out. Soldiers had been stationed inside the Council House, and when the Comanches resisted being taken to jail, the soldiers began firing. In the melee that followed many of the Comanche as well as some whites were killed.

After the slaughter, white captives that had not been fully assimilated into the Comanche culture were tortured and killed. Had the Texans understood and negotiated in good faith, all captives would likely have been returned.

The Comanches were outraged at the betrayal at the hand of the whites. They wanted revenge. Shortly after the slaughter, Buffalo Hump organized the Great Raid of 1840. He and his warrior band razed houses and settlements up and down the frontier from the Edwards Plateau to the Texas Coast. They plundered and killed for years following the Council House incident. Buffalo Hump had finally surrendered in 1846 and was forced onto the reservation in Indian Territory.

Nocona and Shining Rocks were young warriors when they had ridden with Buffalo Hump until near the time of his surrender. A bitter dispute had arisen concerning Buffalo Humps' desire to seek a peace with the Texans. They had left his band, taking a small contingency with them. At times Nocona and his group had joined with Peta Nocona. Over the years they had continued to make small raids upon farms and ranches on the edge of the frontier. Occasionally they would kill white settlers if they were confronted. Nocona had grown less and less satisfied with taking horses and cattle. His desire was for blood.

"The Texans are many, Nocona. Their armies have many rifles and weapons. If we begin to kill whites, they will send their army to kill Comanche. We will all die if we do this thing," said Shining Rocks.

Nocona shook his head in agreement. "You may be right, Shining Rocks. But I have seen that their soldiers no longer ride into our lands. I have heard that they are making war on other whites. If you are right and they come, then we may die. But we will not die like cattle on the white man's reservations. When the Spaniards and Mexicans came, they also tried to make slaves of our people and take our lands. Now the Spaniards and Mexicans are gone. If we show our people that we can resist the whites, then maybe they will unite with us to drive them from our lands. Then they will be gone like the others."

Shining Rocks considered Nocona's words. "I do not fear death, Nocona. And I do not fear the whites. But I do fear being sent to their reservation to live without dignity. So I will fight with you once again. But my spirit tells me that the whites are not like the others. Buffalo Hump had many warriors and now he is gone. Soon, I think, we will be gone."

Nocona stared at the fire and did not reply.

"Will the white trader Mallory have the water that burns?" asked Shining Rocks.

"No, Shining Rocks. We cannot allow our warriors to take the white man's poison. It clouds their minds and makes them weak. We must remain strong and our minds must be set. We will trade only for bullets and weapons."

Nocona turned his attention to his band of warriors and summoned them all to the fire. "Soon we will be ready to make raids on the white man. We have raided his farms and taken his cattle. Now we will make war on his settlements and villages.

His blood will feed the land. When our people see that we can drive the white man out, they will join us and together we will drive the white man from the Comancheria. Then our people will no more live in fear."

The warriors began to shout and whoop.

Nocona looked intently at Shining Rocks. "Now we are ready to avenge our fathers."

Chapter Nine

Keven Mallory was a brutish bully of a man. He liked preying on the weaknesses of other men. He had spent some time in the army, but he had been booted out for drunkenness and continual bad conduct. He had traveled to Texas before the war began and had gone on to do some buffalo hunting. He had later fallen in with more of his kind – thieves, robbers, and brigands. He soon figured out that if he could steal guns, bullets, and other supplies, he could trade and prey upon the needs of the Comanche and other tribes. After recruiting his cousins, he had become successful at building a network of people willing to supply him with information concerning the movement of troops and goods. He soon had a supply of contraband to sell to the natives.

Although he was a drunk and a brute, he was also cunning enough to avoid being caught or positively identified as a gun runner. The rangers suspected that he was supplying guns to the natives, but they seemed to always be a step behind him.

"I'm gonna give that dumb cowboy a bullet for every pain I'm feelin'," Mallory said to his cousins. He touched his broken, bent nose. "If he hadn't sucker punched me, I'd have cut his liver out. He don't know it, but he's gonna see me again. This time I will cut his liver out." He spat into the fire.

He had been drunk when he overheard Hiram and Zeb talking but not so drunk he didn't remember what was said.

"I reckon that cowboy may be carrying money. I heard him mention business at the bank and his friend looked like a man with money. Could be he's doin' something for his fancy friend. Don't matter much. I aim to kill him for what he done to me. If he has money that's even better. And I know where he's headed. We can take care of our business with Nocona and then head to

Fort Graham. Nocona will have horses to trade and we can likely sell them to the army at Fort Graham, and that damned nigger lover is gonna show up there sometime. I can wait him out."

"I hope we got time to visit a whore house," his cousin Deagan spouted. "We lit out of Waco before we had a chance. I fancy that big girl in Waco."

"Now where we gonna find a whore house except back in Waco?" Keegan the second cousin chimed in. "I wish we had brought more whiskey with us. I reckon we'll get some whiskey when we're done with Nocona and that cowboy won't we Keven?" He paused and looked at his cousin. "And I think ya' outta' cut that cowboy's cajones off, Keven. We'll hold him down while ya' do it."

"Naw," Deagan spouted. "I think we should hang that cowboy. Maybe drag him through cactus a good long time first."

"Yeah, we could cut off his eye lids and..."

"Will you two idiots shut the hell up?" Mallory interrupted. "Ain't neither one of you two touching that cowboy. He's all mine. And shut up about the whore house. You keep your mind on business till we're done with Nocona. He's as likely as not to take our scalps after he's done tradin'. I don't trust him, but he'll have horses and maybe hides and money to trade. We can get rid of the horses later without drawing any attention to ourselves. Meanwhile we're stayin' sober and watching our backsides. You two idiots get some sleep. We're heading out tomorrow to where we stashed the wagon with the stuff. You boys got some work to do and I don't want you to be too tired," he said sarcastically. He rubbed the knot on the side of his head and then muttered to himself. "Damned cowboy."

Chapter Ten

Joshua was up before daylight and had coffee brewing. He and Hiram had talked into the night and were growing more comfortable with one another.

"We heading to Fort Graham straight away?" he asked Hiram.

"We will need to go back by the ranch," Hiram replied. "I have one last bit of business to take care of there. We can pick up a pack horse or two and some supplies. We'll be traveling light till then. You have a decent winter coat and a good slicker?"

"You worried I'll get cold and come back home?" Joshua poked at Hiram.

"Nope. I just don't want you trying to crawl under a blanket with me," Hiram retorted.

"In that case I guess I could use a good slicker," Joshua chuckled.

When the coffee was gone the two men readied for the trail. Joshua picked up what few belongings he would take, including his bois d'arc bow. It was a prized possession. Not as good as a rifle at long distance, but quieter and deadly at close range. It was also more effective when trying to take a tasty rabbit for his supper.

When things were properly stowed, the two saddled up. Joshua took a long look around his simple camp. "I hope this don't turn out to be the last mistake I make," he thought to himself.

They followed the Bosque for several hours taking basically the same trail that Hiram had followed to Waco. Both men were silent as they rode. At length, Hiram spoke.

"You got any kin back in Waco?" he asked.

"My mother died a number of years back. The rest of my people had moved on by then. I never knew my father. Did some scouting for the army." He paused for a moment. "I had a wife. She died from a fever."

Neither man spoke for a while.

"You got any family beside your boy?' Joshua asked.

"I've got no one," was Hiram's only reply.

They continued to pick their way along until evening. After they had set up for the night Hiram said casually, "I wish we had seen a nice fat rabbit to take for our supper. I don't mind jerky, but a rabbit would be better."

Joshua said nothing. He picked up his bow and arrows and began to walk toward the edge of the clearing where they were camped.

"Now where in the devil are you going, Joshua?"

"Scoutin'," came the reply as he disappeared into the bush.

Hiram sat sipping a hot cup of coffee when Joshua came walking back into camp carrying two small cottontails. He had been gone no more than thirty minutes.

"How in the world did you manage to take two rabbits in less than an hour?" Hiram questioned.

"Ya' gotta' know where to look. And ya' can't do it with one of those cannons you're shootin'. One shot out of one of those things and there wouldn't be any game left for ten miles." He lifted his bow off of his shoulder and held it out toward Hiram as if to say "you need one of these".

The rabbits were cleaned, fried with salt pork, and consumed. The two men sat with a cup of coffee in hand enjoying the heat of a good fire.

"Joshua, I'm glad you agreed to come along."

"Glad I'm here too Matthews. Anyone can't take a lil' ole rabbit for his supper don't have good survival skills. Needs someone to look after him." Joshua smiled a broad grin.

Later that night the two men lay by the campfire talking.

"Why did you take on the name Joshua instead of.. (Hiram almost said Two Colors before he caught himself) your given name?"

"Didn't like my other name."

Hiram dropped it at that.

"You go by a Christian name now. You a Christian?"

"Don't know that I would say I am. Least ways not how you white men might think. Indians been believing in spirits and a god long before you white men showed up. We call Him the Great Spirit and some other names. You just call Him God. You just dressed Him up some. Why do you ask? You believe in this Christian God, Matthews?"

"Yes, I do, Joshua," Hiram confessed. "And I was just thinking we might need His help before we're done."

On the third day the two men were back at the ranch. The wranglers had not yet returned to the bunk house.

"This was my place until a couple of days ago," he explained to Joshua. "I sold it. That was why I was in Waco. I expect the new owner won't mind us staying here another night. You can stow your gear in the bunk house. There's plenty of room. I'll stay the night in the house."

Joshua sat in the bunk house, still wondering what he was doing when the men returned. He had already grown to like Matthews, and he needed the job, but he still was unsettled about his decision.

Around sundown the men returned to the bunk house. They were unprepared for what they found. And what they found was an Indian, setting on one of the bunks staring at them. The men stood staring at Joshua for several seconds before they were able to speak.

"Who the heck are you, and what are you doing in here." Hank Billings was the first to speak as he unholstered his pistol.

"Hold on white man," Joshua exclaimed. "I'd rather not get shot just now."

"Then you better have a real good story, and you better get to telling it real quick Indian," chimed in Jake Lattimer, the other hired hand.

Aaron was the next to speak. "Mister, I don't know you, and I don't want Hank to shoot you either, but he's right. You picked the wrong place to try to find anything to steal. So, Hank why don't you holster that pistol while we hear just exactly what it is this Indian has to say."

Joshua started to speak just as Hiram walked in to the bunk house. He pointed at Hiram. "Ask him," he said.

"Hank, I think you better put that pistol away before someone gets hurt," Hiram said quickly.

"Boss we walked in on this Indian pilfering for something to steal," Jake interjected.

"Fellows there has been a real misunderstanding here. This is Joshua and he's working for me."

The three men were speechless and stood with their mouths open for a moment. Jake was finally able to speak again.

"Boss, I don't know what's going on here, but you know that me and Hank won't work with no Indian."

"Fellows, I apologize for springing this on all of you. I hired Joshua in Waco. He's going to be helping me with something I have to do. Aaron knows all about it, and I guess I should have told you all before I rode off to Waco. Take a seat. I have something to tell you."

Hiram related the entire story to the men. They sat silent as he explained the sale of the ranch and his intentions. When he finished, the men remained silent as the whole story sank in.

"Will has agreed to keep you men on here. Nothing will change much for you fellows."

"This ain't right, Hiram," Jake finally spoke. "We've been with you a while now and it don't seem right what you're sayin'. I mean, we can all work for Will. I know him, and I don't mind the idea of workin' for him, but it don't seem right."

"You men are free to do what you feel is right for you. I can't tell you what to do. I hope you'll think about it. I only know what I have to do, and the deal is done." Hiram said. "Joshua and I will be heading up to Fort Graham after we pull together what we need."

"Well I guess there's not much else to say then boss," Hank offered. "But I think Jake feels the same as me, and I ain't stayin' under the same roof with no Indian."

Joshua sensed a real split brewing and chimed in. "I don't want to cause trouble here, so if it's all the same to you fellows, I'll stay in the barn tonight. I believe that will work best for everyone, Matthews."

"Then I guess that's it fellows," Hiram said. The strange assembly stood silent for a moment. Hiram offered his hand to the men. "Best of luck," he said as he shook their hands.

Aaron followed Hiram from the bunk house and Joshua headed for the barn. "Hiram, I need to talk to you," he said. "I've been thinking. You're not just my boss. You're my friend. I don't believe that you need to go it alone on this. I know you have the Indian now to help you out. I can't say that I like that idea. First sign of trouble and he's likely to light out. And I guess that him being along sort of changes things, but.... well, what I'm trying to say is I think you should take me along with you. If that Indian takes off, you'll be out there by yourself. If you run into a scrape you could use another man. I can't say I'd be the best man in a scrape, but I can handle a rifle if I'm not rushed."

"Aaron, you're putting me on the spot here," Hiram replied. "I truly wouldn't mind having someone along that I know and trust, but this isn't your duty. I don't know where this thing may take me. I don't like the idea of maybe putting you in danger. All that aside, that probably leaves you without a job. How would you manage that?"

"Will came by to check on things and I spoke with him. He's willing to put me back to work when I come back. I've got a small poke saved up. If you can pick up the essentials, I reckon I'll be okay for a spell," Aaron offered.

"I'll have to sleep on it Aaron. I pulled Joshua into this thing against better judgment. Right now, I just don't think it's a good idea. It's too much to ask of a friend."

"Then we'll talk again in the morning."

Chapter Eleven

Nocona was in no mood for a lot of haggling over the price of the guns and ammunition that Mallory and his cousins had brought to the meeting. Mallory himself was wary of Nocona and sensed that he could lose more than the guns if he angered Nocona and his band. They had met at the prescribed place and time. Mallory had looked over the horses and hides that Nocona had brought. He was prepared to make a quick deal and put as much territory as possible between him and the fierce looking bunch. Nocona and his men were out for blood, and they didn't much care what white man it was.

Mallory spoke through Nocona's interpreter. "One gun for each brave and one hundred-fifty rounds of ammunition," Mallory offered. "We take all the horses and hides. And I'll throw in two bottles of whiskey." Offering the whiskey was a mistake.

Nocona's face grew ever more grim.

"Offer your poison again and I will take your scalp and your guns," Nocona replied. "We will take the guns and 200 rounds of ammunition."

"We've done too much business over the years to allow my little gesture to come between you and what you need, Nocona. But I know you have the white man's coins and the paper with drawings. Show me the paper and maybe we make a trade."

Nocona motioned to Shining Rocks and pointed to the small pouch that hung at his waist. Shining Rocks dumped the contents. Mallory counted the bills and coins. "The guns and ammunition for the hides, horses, and the paper and coins." Mallory offered.

"Take the paper with the white man's drawings," Nocona replied. "I do not understand its worth."

Mallory signaled agreement and instructed his cousins to unload the rifles and ammunition. "Be quick about it before he changes his mind and decides to kill us all," he told his cousins. "String those horses together and get those hides loaded. I want to leave here with all my parts."

When the wagon was loaded Mallory and his cousins wasted no time in getting on the move. They didn't slow down until they felt they had put a safe distance between themselves and Nocona.

"Now we got some unfinished business," Mallory informed his cousins. "We'll drop these ponies back where we keep the wagon. We'll sell 'em later. We push hard for Fort Graham. I want to be there before that damn cowboy shows up. I've got a friend I need to talk to."

The trio had made good speed and reached the high bank of the Brazos overlooking Fort Graham. From that position it was possible to keep an eye on the river crossing to the fort side of the river. Mallory only hoped that Hiram had not yet arrived and that he would come this way.

"We camp here," he instructed his cousins. "If that cowboy hasn't made it yet, we might spot him from here. I figure he'll be along in a day or two."

"I hope they have whiskey down there," Deagan spoke up. "And maybe a whore."

"We'll get whiskey but we stay sober till my business is done with that cowboy," Mallory said. "We stay here for now. I don't want to run into that cowboy by accident. Keegan, I want you to ride into the fort. I doubt that cowboy will remember you, but he would recognize me. Find a fella named Ham Buckner. Tell him I need to talk to him. Ask around and probably anyone can point you in his direction. Bring him back here and bring back some whiskey."

Ham Buckner was as mean as Mallory, and sly. He was a thief and was always on the lookout for an unsuspecting traveler upon whom he could prey. But he would kill to rob someone of nothing more than a dollar or two. He was the sort that could gather information, and Mallory needed someone in the fort watching. If Hiram had come and gone, Buckner would know. If he was behind them, Buckner could find out where he was headed when he left the fort.

It took Keegan a good portion of the day to find Buckner and bring him back to the camp.

"Your man told me you was up here, Mallory. We brought some whiskey like you said. What's up?"

"I've got a little job I need you to do for me. I'm lookin' for a man, and if you can help me find him there's a gold piece in it for you. I've got a score to settle with him," Mallory said. "He's gonna be looking for a ranger named Walker."

"I know Walker," Ham replied.

"That's good. You hang close to him and you'll find this cowboy. Name's Hiram something," Mallory instructed. He then described Hiram as best he could.

"If he comes to the fort, I'll know it. Ain't but a few people passed through here recently. From your description I'm thinkin' he ain't come through yet."

"I need to know where he's headed when he leaves the fort. That's all I need you to find out," Mallory growled.

Chapter Twelve

Hiram was up long before daylight. He had slept little. He had tried all night to convince himself that having Aaron along was a bad idea. He had run all the possibilities over and over. A hundred things could happen and ninety-eight of them could end badly. But the need to have a man along that he could trust weighed heavily on him. He sat drinking coffee in the kitchen of the ranch house for what would likely be the last time. He was deep in thought again when he heard Aaron tap lightly on the door.

"You up in here," Aaron called softly as he opened the door.

Hiram was at the table pouring his friend a cup of coffee. "Come on in Aaron," he called.

After they were seated at the table he looked at Aaron and shared his thoughts. "You cost me a lot of sleep last night Aaron. I've mulled this thing over a thousand times. If you've really thought this through, I'm willing to let you ride along to Fort Graham. If my search takes me into any kind of potential danger, you're out. If you're willing to give me your word that you'll abide by that, then you're in as far as Fort Graham."

"Then we have a deal, Hiram. It's the right decision."

By noon the three men were ready to ride. The supplies were loaded and Hiram had cut out a fresh mount for Joshua. He preferred that they all be well mounted, and the nag that Joshua was riding didn't suit Hiram.

They bid their goodbyes and by shortly after noon they were headed to Fort Graham. Joshua and Aaron had not spoken a word to one another. The tension between the two men was apparent. Aaron didn't trust Indians and Joshua didn't trust most white men. The trio rode in relative silence for most of the day. Aaron was the first to attempt to cut the tension.

"I never rode with an Indian before," he suddenly offered.

"I never did either," Joshua replied. "Don't trust em."

Aaron was silent for a moment. Then out of the blue he began to laugh.

An hour before sundown the trio camped in a small clearing and made preparations for the night. After supper the men sat silent around a small campfire.

"How long before we reach Fort Graham?" Aaron inquired of Hiram.

"I expect day after tomorrow," Hiram replied. "I hope to find Ranger Walker there. He led the hunt for Ethan when he was taken. If nothing else he should be able to supply me with information about the Comanches. If Ethan was taken by Indians, it was likely Comanches that took him. Walker might have information about any trades or ransom of captives. It's a stretch, but it's all I've got."

"It's been a long time since your son was taken, Hiram. You really think he might have been sold or ransomed?"

"That's my hope Aaron. I know that has been common practice with the Comanches. Maybe Ethan was sold back to a white settlement somewhere. I don't know."

"But if he had been ransomed wouldn't he have been identified and brought home?" Aaron inquired.

"Not if he had his tongue cut out," Joshua interjected. "Comanches don't treat hostages with any great tenderness. They got meaner after Council House. A lot of white children were kept and became part of their bands before that betrayal. After that they took to killing and torturing captives."

"I don't know anything about this Council House," Hiram said. "And I don't want to hear any more talk about that sort of thing. Find something else to talk about."

"Just being realistic about things, Matthews," Joshua replied. "Maybe your boy is alive. But finding him's gonna be like trying to touch the moon."

"Then I'll have to touch the moon," Hiram replied. "Let's get some sleep."

The next morning broke cool and clear. The trio rode silently through most of the day. Small talk seemed pointless after the previous evening's discussion. They kept a steady course north toward the Brazos River. None of the three had ever been as far north as Fort Graham but Joshua, who was now leading the way, knew that if they made the Brazos they could follow it to the settlement.

Fort Graham was one of several forts built along what was at that time the edge of the frontier. It had now become a small settlement. The river was prone to flooding in wet years and the fort was built on the highest land on the north side. The trio had followed the Brazos and could now see the fort from their perch on the high bank of the river opposite the fort.

"We'll camp down there somewhere near the fort," Hiram informed the two. "Tomorrow we'll find Walker if he's there."

Chapter Thirteen

Hiram and his companions rode into Fort Graham the next morning. He was anxious to find the ranger. He stopped the first citizen he saw. "I'm looking for a ranger named Walker," he said.

"I know Ranger Walker," the man replied. "Rangers have a small building outside the old fort at the north end of the settlement. That's where you'll find him if he's here. You probably saw the building when you rode in. Not but a few buildings and his is the last one." He pointed a thumb to the north.

The three men tied their horses to the rail outside the building.

"You want us to go in with you?" Aaron inquired.

"I do," Hiram replied. "You need to know what you're getting yourself into, and I want you to hear what Walker has to say."

Walker was seated at a small table when the three entered. He stood and addressed the men. "Something I can do for you fellows? I'm Sam Walker." He rounded the table and stuck out a hand.

"Ranger Walker, I'm Hiram Matthews and this is Aaron Russel, and Joshua. I doubt you remember me. We met a number of years ago. You were dispatched when my son disappeared over near Waco."

"I thought your face was familiar. I do remember," Walker replied. "We suspected that your boy was taken by Indians. Never found a trace. You men take a seat." He pointed to several small chairs. "So, what brings you to Fort Graham?"

"I don't want to put too fine a point on it, but I'm determined to try to find my boy."

Walker leaned back in his chair and studied Hiram's face for a moment.

"Well, that's straight to the point all right. Why now? It's been seven or eight years as best I recall."

"Yes sir," Hiram replied. "It's been about that long. I don't need to go into my reasons. I'm here to see if there is anything you can tell me."

"I guess I'm at a bit of a loss as to what it is that you think I can tell you. I remember that we searched around your place looking for your son. Thought maybe he was just lost. We finally found some personal item belonging to your son. Maybe a play thing. I don't remember for sure."

"It was a toy pistol that I had carved for the boy," Hiram interjected.

"We found it down by the creek and there were pony tracks there. Looked to be a small band. The tracks were from unshod ponies, and I believe that led us to think that maybe your son had been abducted by Indians. We tried following their trail, but I remember that we lost any trace."

"I believe that is a just account of what happened," Hiram replied.

"Then I'm still at a loss as to what else it is that I can add, Mr. Matthews."

"I know that the Comanches have taken and sold back captives. I was hoping you might have information of any trades or ransoms that were paid for white captives around that time."

"There have been a few captives sold back to their families over the years. I'm sure that I can't know of every instance," Walker countered. "I know that Buffalo Hump was the most notorious for that. But he surrendered back in forty-six, and all captives that he held were returned to their families as far as I know."

"Were there others?" Hiram inquired.

"Well, there were a few others; that is, that we know. Most have been captured and sent off to the Territory or killed. There's one band led by an Indian named Nocona. He's never been captured. There's little we know of him. He and a small band have continued to make raids up and down the frontier. Been seen by no more than a few living whites. His band has been responsible for a number of thefts and a few killings. Or at least we suspect it's him. If you're thinking of chasing the like of him down to find your son, I will strongly advise against it."

"I'm not sure what I'm thinking right now," Hiram replied.

"Look Mr. Matthews, here's the truth of it. Many of the bad Comanches have been pushed well back into the Comancheria. Smallpox and cholera have reduced their numbers. Many of their bands have been moved north to Indian Territory. There are a few bands living up around the Wichita and Pease. They're mostly friendly and pretty much have always been. If your son was kept – and that's a big if - it's possible that he was taken up there. They've been known to trade for captives with some of their less friendly cousins. Then they turn around and try to ransom them back to the white settlers or the army. There are still isolated bands of Kiowa and Comanche like Nocona's bunch and you don't want to tangle with any of those. They mostly seem to stay on the outer reaches of the western frontier. If you stick to the interior you should be okay. If you really believe that your son might actually be alive, I suggest that you stay well away from the Comancheria and start with the bands up north on the Wichita or maybe in the territory. But you've got to know that hoping to find your son will be like looking for the needle in a hay stack. Personally, I doubt that your son survived. I don't mean to offend you. That's just the hard reality."

"Go ahead and shoot him," Joshua muttered under his breath.

"What was that?" Walker asked.

"Just mumbling to myself," Joshua replied. Hiram gave him a stern look.

"I appreciate your time Ranger Walker. I'm bound to see this through. The bunch up on the Wichita is as good a place to start as any."

The ranger could hardly believe that anyone would hope to accomplish such a thing without any solid indications of where to actually start. "If you're bent on riding north to the Wichita, I suggest you stick to the south side of the river for a day or so. Going's easier." Walker offered. He rose and went to a crude map on the back wall of the office. "We're right here on the map. Fort Worth is about fifty miles nearly due north of here on the Trinity about right here. The Wichita is northwest of there. You can follow the Brazos west toward Fort Cooper up near the headwaters. The Pease is north of there. That's where you'll find the Comanche camps. The army and settlers have been pushing the edge of the frontier steadily west. You probably noticed there aren't many troops here any more. They all moved to Cooper and some of the Confederate forts. Things changed when Texas seceded. I have paper if you want to make yourself a map."

The three men rode back to their camp in silence. They were still unaware that they had been carefully watched by Ham Buckner. Buckner had sneaked to the back of the ranger office and had pressed his ear against a crack in the wall. He hadn't heard everything, but he heard enough to know the men would be going northwest from the fort. That would take them back across the river where the trail would be easiest.

Mallory and his henchmen cousins were waiting when Ham rode into their camp.

"I think I might have some interesting news for you," he told Mallory. "There was a cowboy rode into the fort today. He went straight to the ranger office. Looks like the man you described, but he wasn't alone. Had two others with him."

"Damn," Mallory replied. "Must be the bunch we saw. You sure it's him?"

"Sure as I can be," Buckner replied. "Heard 'em say they was going north. They'll be coming back across the river."

"Then we'll be watching for 'em when they cross. And you better be right on this."

Chapter Fourteen

The trio of cutthroats watched from the high bank overlooking the river as Aaron, Hiram, and Joshua crossed back to the south side of the river. They had passed within two hundred yards of Mallory and his cousins when they rode in. The cutthroats had seen the three men cross the river, but paid them little attention. They were looking for a lone cowboy.

"We'll follow them till tonight," Malory told his cousins. "There's good light from the moon and we'll wait till they're asleep. Then we'll hit 'em. I want that cowboy alive. He ends up dead; I'll have your hides. They ain't expecting us so this ought to be easy. We take 'em all alive if we can. Might be able to sell the others to Nocona or some other bunch. The Indian ain't important though. I'll let you two have him when I'm done with the cowboy if you want to cut him up. But Nocona might like to have a white man to boil in hides."

Hiram, Joshua, and Aaron had chosen a camp site under a large stand of live oak trees. Joshua had grown a bit jittery during the day.

"Just the strange company and territory," Hiram had thought. It seemed that Mallory was right. No one suspected what was to befall them.

Mallory and his cousins had followed at a safe distance throughout the day. They estimated that the trio had bedded down for the night about a half mile ahead of them. They lagged back until just before dark and made their way cautiously toward their unsuspecting victims. They could smell the smoke from the campfire when Mallory halted. He signaled his cousins to remain quiet and dismounted. He huddled them closely and gave instructions.

"I figure they're camped a couple hundred yards straight ahead. Keegan, you take the horses back about a hundred yards and tie 'em up good. Don't want a noisy mount to give us away. We'll wait here for you. When the moons up we'll hit 'em. Shouldn't need to fire a shot long as we're quiet. We'll hold 'em till morning. Then that damn cowboy gets what he's got coming. A bullet won't do. I got somethin' real special in mind." One of the horses whinnied softly. "Get that damned horse out of here like I told ya before they hear us."

The moon rose fairly bright. The trio of cutthroats had crept closer and could make out the shadowy images of the men preparing to bed down for the night. They hadn't made a sound.

Deagan leaned in close to Mallory and whispered, "I don't see but two of em."

"Third one's probably takin' a squirt," Mallory hissed. "We'll wait till they're asleep. We go in quiet like and don't make a sound. We can disarm 'em without firin' a shot."

The trio waited another thirty minutes then began to creep into the camp. They finally found themselves standing directly over the sleeping men. Keegan and Deagan had a rifle and a shotgun trained at Aaron and Joshua. Mallory quietly shoved his rifle muzzle against Hiram's throat. Hiram awoke with a jolt and felt the cold steel at his throat.

"Get on your feet Cowboy," Mallory growled as he kicked hard at the ribs of the man under the blankets. Hiram was stunned and winded by the kick and rolled to one knee.

"Remember me cowboy? We met back in Waco. Now you're gonna pay for what you done to me." Mallory turned to his cousins. Aaron had gotten to his feet still sleepy-eyed and confused by what was taking place. Deagan kicked at the blankets covering Joshua. He felt no resistance and reached down and jerked the blankets back. There was no one there, only another rolled up blanket and horse blanket.

"That damn Indian ain't here," he declared. The three men were surprised to find him gone and began to scan the area with their eyes straining against the low light.

"No matter," Mallory said. "He probably lit out on these two to go back to his squaw or something. He's anywhere out there and sees what's happening he ain't comin' back." Mallory turned his attention to Aaron and Hiram.

"Tie these two's hands. We're gonna hoist 'em up on one of these oaks. Pull 'em up by their wrists till their toes just touch the ground good. I don't want 'em to suffocate. I just want to make sure they're real uncomfortable. And don't worry about hurting 'em. Keegan, you'll stand watch, and Deagan will spell you in a few hours just in case that Indian shows back up. We'll get some shut eye. I need to be rested so I can work on this cowboy in the morning. And get that whiskey from my saddle bag." He looked down at Hiram and let fly a hard kick to Hiram's face and then another to his ribs. Aaron was standing and Keegan slammed his shotgun butt hard into Aaron's ribs. Aaron went to his knees and Deagan slammed his rifle butt into Aaron's head.

"Throw your ropes over one of these oak limbs and string these two up like I said," Mallory growled. "Make sure they can breathe. I want that cowboy alive and well in the morning."

Hiram was dazed and once his head began to clear he realized that he and Aaron were hanging by their wrists. Hiram could see the three men at the fire. They were drinking whiskey and talking. Hiram's face felt like he had been kicked by a horse. He looked toward Aaron and saw that he was barely conscious.

"You hurt badly?" he asked.

"My ribs hurt really bad. Hard to breathe," Aaron gasped.

Hiram shook his head trying to get the fog from his brain. He looked around as best he could. He didn't see Joshua. He immediately assumed that their assailants had killed him. He turned back to Aaron.

"Can you hold out a while?" he asked.

"Don't know. Can't catch my breath good. Hurts like sin," Aaron mumbled.

Hiram realized that Aaron might not see the daylight if he hung there all night. He called out to the men.

"You men want my friend dead by morning you leave him where he is. You want him alive you better cut him down. He'll suffocate before morning."

"I don't give a hoot in hell if your friend dies. Ain't nuthin' to me," Mallory scoffed.

Keegan chimed in. "You said we could sell that cowboy to the Indians. He dies, we lose that money Mallory."

Mallory rubbed his chin. "You want him down, you get to stay awake and watch him. I'm getting some sleep," he growled.

"Me and Deagan watch him, we get to split whatever we get for him," Keegan declared.

"Don't matter to me," Mallory replied.

Keegan and Deagan looked at one another and hurriedly went to cut Aaron down. They bound his feet and dumped him at Hiram's feet.

Hiram lost all concept of time. His side hurt. He didn't know how long he had been hanging, but he felt like his lungs would burst and his arms burned like fire. He discovered that he could stand on tip toe and breathe a bit better. He finally began to lose consciousness.

Light began to show through the trees and struck Hiram in the face. He awakened slowly. His whole body was racked with pain. Keegan and his cousin were asleep by the fire and Mallory was beginning to stir. Hiram looked down at Aaron, and he could tell he was still breathing. He had no idea what Mallory intended to do to him, but the thought brought chills. He hadn't figured on dying at the hands of a bar room bully.

Presently Mallory rolled onto his back and sat up. He wiped his eyes with the back of his hands and looked around. He saw Keegan and Deagan sleeping by the fire and shook his head. He rose and kicked Deagan. Deagan let out a howl and sprang to his feet. Keegan sat up suddenly, and Mallory took a kick at him.

"I told you two to stay awake and watch that cowboy you cut down. That damn Indian could have come in here and cut our throats if he were around. I've a mind to give you both a beatin'. Lucky for you two idiots I've got other business. Now see if these two have any more coffee with them," Mallory commanded.

Mallory strode over to Hiram and gave him a hard whack across the face with the back of his hand.

"Recognize me, cowboy? I recognize you and I've got something real special planned for you. I'm gonna skin you like a rabbit. But I'm gonna do it real slow so ya don't die on me. May take a day or two. You're real strong. That's good. Keeps you alive longer. But I'm gonna hurt ya' real bad for suckering me like ya' did."

Hiram shuddered from the pain and the prospect of what was to come. He was in a fix with no way out.

Mallory walked back to the fire and withdrew a skinning knife from its sheath. He tested the edge and grinned. Keegan picked up his shotgun and laid it across his folded arm. Deagan stood to his side. The business end of the shotgun was aimed in his direction, and Deagan paid no attention.

"This is gonna be good. Mallory knows how to skin anything. Never seen him skin a man," Keegan declared. Deagan laughed and stamped his feet as though he were a child about to get a piece of candy. Mallory poured himself a cup of coffee.

"When I tell ya', you two hoist that cowboy up a bit and move his friend outta' my way," he commanded.

He stood sipping his coffee for a bit. Then he walked over and stood in front of Hiram.

"This knife is plenty sharp. You'll hardly feel me peeling your skin back at first," he said. He grabbed Hiram's shirt and tore it back from his chest. "I'll make me a little cut right across here," he said as he drew the back of the knife across Hiram's chest. "Then I'll make another here." He continued to outline the cuts with the back of the knife. "Then we'll be ready to see how tough you are cowboy." He motioned for the cousins to pull Hiram higher and to move Aaron.

He laid the sharp edge to Hiram's chest and began to make a shallow cut across Hiram's skin. Hiram began to shake trying to move away from the blade, but movement only made the knife cut deeper.

Keegan and Deagan had not moved and were watching what was happening like rabid dogs. Keegan still had the shotgun laid across his folded arm. He never saw or felt the arrow until it pierced his neck, severing his jugular vein. He let out a muffled, gurgling scream as blood filled his throat. The impact of the arrow and the sudden surprise caused him to squeeze the trigger of the shotgun. The gun erupted, and the blast caught Deagan fully in the face. His face and most of his head disappeared and he fell dead. Keegan was wildly pulling at the arrow and blood was spewing from his neck. He collapsed and lay writhing on the ground. Mallory spun and sprinted to his rifle. He scanned the surrounding brush wildly. The next arrow found purchase in his shoulder. He dropped his rifle and screamed wildly and grabbed at the embedded arrow. A second arrow hit him in his stomach. He let out another scream and began to wretch. He collapsed to the ground clutching the arrow in his stomach. Blood and vomit filled his throat.

Hiram was thrashing from side to side trying to see and comprehend what was taking place. He saw no one. He spun himself around on the rope just as Joshua walked from the brush.

"Looks like you were in a tight spot Matthews," he declared calmly. "Told ya you lacked good survival skills."

"Never so glad to see a smart ass Indian in my whole life," Hiram said grimly. "Cut me down quick. I feel like I'm near dead."

Joshua released the rope at its binding and Hiram collapsed in a heap. He felt as though his arms were mush. Joshua knelt at Aaron's side and rolled him onto his back. He turned to Hiram. "Your friend's alive. Don't know how badly he's hurt. He ain't bleeding anywhere I can see."

Hiram finally managed to sit up.

"I was afraid you were dead when I didn't see you. Where the devil were you?"

"Yesterday I had a feeling we were being followed. Don't ask me why. I felt it more than I knew it. About the time we laid down, I was almost certain I heard a horse whinny. Maybe it's an Indian thing. After you bedded down I fixed my bedroll to make it look like I was there and belly crawled into the brush. Good thing I had my bow. Never counted on that damn fool blowing the other one's head off like that. May be the best shot I ever made."

Aaron was beginning to moan a bit and appeared to be regaining consciousness. Hiram crawled on hands and knees to his side. He could feel his arms a little. He patted Aaron's cheeks to rouse him.

"Am I dead?" Aaron moaned as he came to.

"Not today," Hiram said as he winced. "You've probably got broken ribs though. Can you sit up yet?"

"Let me lay a spell, my heads clearing some."

"Help me up Joshua," Hiram said as he extended an arm.

Hiram was still unsteady on his feet but was able to walk to where Keegan and Deagan lay. Both men were dead. He turned his attention to Mallory. The man was still writhing in pain as he clutched the arrow in his belly. Hiram could feel his anger rising.

"Your men dead and my friend hurt over a stupid thing like a fist fight. I can't understand a man like you mister," he said angrily. Mallory did not reply.

"Let's get you down by the fire and get some coffee in you," Joshua interjected. "I'll get your friend up and get him over here too."

When Joshua had the two men resting by the fire he felt a need to explain something. "I'm sorry I had to wait so long to act. I couldn't take a chance in the dark. I was as likely to hit one of you as one of them. Sorry he cut you before I could get a clear shot, Matthews."

"No need to explain yourself to me," said Hiram." "If it weren't for you they would have killed both of us."

"So what do you want me to do with the two dead ones?" Joshua asked.

"Give me a bit to get my feet under me, and I'll help you round up some stones to cover them. Can't bury them in this rocky ground. Besides, we don't have a shovel."

"What about the other one?" Joshua asked again.

"I don't fancy putting a bullet in him. Let him lay. It isn't the Christian thing to do, I know. But his fate's his own now. If he dies before we can get ourselves pulled together, we'll cover him like the others."

"What about your friend? He don't look so good."

"I don't see we have any choice but to take him back to Fort Graham. He may be hurt inside. Maybe we can get some help there. Can you make a travois to carry him? Darned if this isn't bad luck being followed by this bunch."

A short while later the two dead bodies were covered and Mallory was still alive. He was semi-conscious and had begun to beg for the men to shoot him.

"I'll not waste a bullet on the likes of you," Hiram said. His conscience stung a bit when he said it.

Two hours later the trio was loaded and ready to head back to Ft. Graham. Hiram took a last look at Mallory and headed his mare toward the fort.

Chapter Fifteen

Nocona and his band were ready to shed more blood. They had made their way steadily north after acquiring the guns and ammunition from Mallory. They had skirted the edge of the frontier looking for easy prey to whet the thirst of their band for more blood. There had been two unsuspecting settler families that had been unfortunate enough to find themselves in their path. They had tortured and killed the two farmers and their families. There were seven dead in their wake. Now they were surveying a third family.

Nocona and Shining Rocks crouched silently in the brush on a hillside watching smoke rise from the chimney of the sod and log cabin. They saw the man busily harnessing his plow mules. The man's wife was still inside the cabin.

Nocona watched intently as the man led his team toward an already developed field. It was late fall and the man was readying to prepare the ground for spring. Nocona turned to Shining Rocks.

"This white man, he thinks he will have corn to feed his children this summer. There will be no corn. There will be no white man. Only his bones and the ashes of his dwelling," he said to Shining Rocks.

"We have killed only a few white men and their families since Mallory sold us the rifles. This man is like the others. He breaks our land and has no fear of us," Shining Rocks replied.

"When our warriors have tasted more blood they will be ready to raid the white man's villages. Then we will kill many and they will know fear. But today we will kill this fool. We will rape his woman and burn his children." The two turned silently and crept back to their horses.

"We will wait until the man is in the field. He will be distracted by his work. Then we will kill him. He has the mules. Make sure we do not harm them. We will take those to keep for trade. Maybe we keep his woman when the warriors are through with her," Nocona instructed Shining Rocks.

The settler had his plow in the ground and struggled to keep it biting. He had spent weeks piling the stones that overturned each time he plowed. But he was making progress he told himself. He was hoping to plant food crops for him and his wife. He had the cow for milk, and if he could have a small garden close to the cabin he would have potatoes and a few other vegetables that would keep in a root cellar. He was feeling pretty good about things. His wife hadn't been happy when he had decided to break off from the other four settlers. "It's not safe," she had told him. She had begged him to stay with the group to pool their efforts and to provide a greater level of protection and safety. He had been adamant about making it on his own. The decision would cost him his life.

The settler halted his mule team and was wiping his brow when Nocona and some of his men burst into the field. The man stood frozen as though he didn't comprehend what was taking place. The first warrior ran by the man at a gallop. The chest of his mount clipped the farmer and knocked him to the ground. Before he could recover several others were on him with their knives drawn. He was stabbed repeatedly before he fully realized what was happening. He lay on his back. He looked up at his assailants and muttered, "There aren't supposed to be Indians in these parts any more." His eyes blinked rapidly as his blood pooled on the ground. The darkness enveloped him.

The rest of the band had dragged the woman from the cabin and had partially torn her clothing away. They were taunting her, jabbing her with the muzzles of their weapons and whipping her with rawhide thongs as she clutched at her clothing. They shoved her from man to man as they whooped and hollered. When they tired of their games, they dragged her back into the cabin. Several of the warriors entered and exited the building in turns. Her screams finally ceased.

"Take the cattle and mules," Nocona finally commanded Shining Rocks. "If the woman is alive, bring her. Burn the white man's dwelling."

The woman was dragged by her hair from the cabin as it was being torched. She was barely able to stand and was in shock. She was wild-eyed and began to whimper in German. "Where's my Albert. I want my Albert."

"What is this strange language that the woman speaks?" Shining Rocks asked Nocona.

"She is talking a spirit language. Maybe she speaks with the man's spirit," Nocona replied. "She may be a witch." The warriors standing near the woman heard Nocona speak and withdrew several steps.

"Leave her here. She will bring evil spirits to our camp. If we try to kill her she may turn herself into a wolf and kill us in our sleep," Nocona commanded.

The assembled band of warriors rode away to the northwest leaving the crazed woman standing alone staring at the burning cabin. She was whimpering over and over, "Where did you go, Albert? Where are you?"

Nocona and his band had ridden for two days after killing the farmer. The warriors had been murmuring among themselves. They were fearful. They had harmed the witch and were afraid she would come into their camp and kill them in their sleep. As they sat at their fire one warrior asked Nocona what could be done.

"It is a serious thing to harm a witch. If we had killed her she would come as a spirit and enter our minds to poison us. She may have already placed a spell on us. I think we should smoke and ask the spirits of our ancestors to come and protect us from this witch. Those who touched her need to be cleansed. We should wash in the stream and build a sweat lodge. Each man must wash and enter the lodge and speak with the fathers."

"When we are cleansed will we make war on the white man's villages?" Shining Rocks asked Nocona.

"We will ride to the river in the north where Peta Nocona was killed by the whites. There are villages of our people there. When they hear that the white soldiers are gone, maybe they will join us."

Chapter Sixteen

Hiram and Joshua continued riding into the night. Aaron's condition had not improved, but had not seemed to grow worse and he was conscious off and on. They reached the fort just around day break and pulled up in front of the fort's headquarter office. A soldier standing on the porch stepped down to examine the man on the travois.

"My friend is hurt. He may have broken ribs. Maybe worse. Is there a doctor here?" Hiram asked.

"We've got a man trained some but he's not a doctor. Nearest doctor will be up in Ft. Worth," the soldier replied. "We do have an infirmary. It's right over there," the soldier pointed.

Joshua and Hiram helped Aaron onto a cot in the infirmary. The corporal in charge came over and asked a few questions. After a brief exam, he offered his opinion.

"Your man does have a couple of broken ribs. I don't think he has serious internal injuries. He took a pretty bad blow to the head. I'm just not well trained enough to make any judgments there. He's going to need bed rest for a while, and he won't be able to do much for at least several weeks. We can keep him here in the infirmary for now. I'll need to check with the Captain to clear it," the corporal said.

"I'll be glad to pay for any expense," Hiram told the young Corporal.

"You can speak with the Captain about all that. The Private will take you to him."

Captain Hamilton Baines was an army regular and popular with his small command. His men respected and admired him. He was firm when needed but could also be understanding and compassionate.

The Private led Hiram to the Captain's office and asked him to wait. He knocked and entered. After a few moments the Captain exited.

"I understand you brought in an injured man. Is he seriously injured?" the Captain asked.

"Your Corporal said he probably has a few broken ribs," Hiram replied.

"Painful injuries. I instructed the Private to make sure that his needs are met. It looks as though you need some attention as well."

"I'll be fine. I can cover any expenses for Mr. Russel's care, but I'm in a bit of a jam," Hiram informed the Captain. "I'll need to leave him until he is well enough to travel. I'm bound for the Wichita, and I can't sit around here for a month waiting for him to mend."

"We can make arrangements for all that," Baines replied. He studied Hiram for a moment. His eyes suddenly widened. "I believe you were here just a day or two ago were you not?"

"That's right," Hiram replied. "We were set upon by three men just a day's ride out from here. There's a story there, but I won't bore you with it."

"Was anyone else injured?" the Captain inquired.

"No one else in my party. I'm cut and beat up a bit, but I'm fine. I can't say the same for the three men. Two are dead and the third is likely dead by now."

"Then I think you will need to come into my office and tell me what happened, Mr....."

"Hiram Matthews."

"I'm Captain Hamilton Baines, Mr. Matthews," he said as they walked into his small office. "If you will, tell me exactly what happened." The men took a seat and Hiram related the entire story to the Captain. At the end of the account, he added his thoughts.

"I don't even know their names. The leader of the bunch was a really brutal man. Had a big scar across the side of his face." He drew his finger across his own cheek. "I believe I heard one of the others call him Malloy. Something like that."

Captain Baines leaned back in his chair and shook his head in disbelief. "That would be Kevin Mallory and his cousins," he replied. "We know of him well. The army and the rangers have been after him for a while. He is suspected of supplying guns to the natives. He's not the type to work and he always seemed to have ponies or hides to sell. But we could never catch him red-handed. Did he have weapons with him?"

"None that we can say," Hiram replied.

"You fellows are lucky to be alive. Brutal is a good description of him."

"It was touch and go, Captain. We owe our lives to my other companion."

"I'll need to inform Walker of all this. He'll be grateful that a bad bunch has been stopped. You men probably have saved countless lives. I'll have the Private put you up here tonight. Don't worry about your friend. He will be in good hands."

"I've need to speak with my friend so I'll take my leave and go back to the infirmary if that's all right."

Aaron was awake when Hiram returned. He pulled a chair to the cot and took a seat.

"I understand that you will live," he stated grimly. "But your ride with me and Joshua is done. We agreed on this back at the ranch. You can't travel, and I can't wait. I'll be leaving you here. Captain Baines will see to your needs until you can travel. It's only a few days' ride back to the ranch. Maybe Walker will see to it that you get back safely. I'll speak with him. I am sorry that I dang nearly got you killed. It was bad luck you being with me when those three showed up. I won't take that chance again."

"I'm sorry I can't help you finish this Hiram," Aaron stated. There was genuine sorrow in his voice. "I believe that you've got a good man with you. Joshua's all right."

Hiram patted his friend's shoulder. "That's it then, Aaron. I'll drop by in the morning on the way out."

The two men shook hands for what they both knew could be the last time.

Chapter Seventeen

The two crossed the Brazos and were headed steadily northwest along the river for two days. They avoided the spot where Mallory and his cousins had attacked them. Had they checked they would have found that Mallory's body was gone. There was no way for them to know of the two buffalo hunters who had happened upon Mallory and loaded the critically wounded man into their wagon.

On the morning of the third day, Joshua rode ahead of Hiram a short distance. Hiram was watching his tracks as he followed along behind. After several hours, he looked up to see Joshua returning at a gallop.

"There's a little valley about a mile ahead. Looks like a burned out cabin down there," he reported.

"Probably some settler's abandoned place."

"I don't think so, Matthews. There's a small crop field and it's partially plowed. Bunch of buzzards feeding on something in the field. I can't be sure, but I think it's a body."

"Let's have a look. Could still be someone down there that needs help."

The two picked their way through the brush until they came to the spot where Joshua had seen the remnants of the cabin. The buzzards were still feeding.

"Let's get down there quick," Hiram said.

When they approached the field it became apparent that the buzzards were feeding on a corpse. The two men halted at the edge of the brush. Hiram drew his pistol to fire a shot to scare the buzzards away. Joshua reached over and grabbed Hiram by his arm.

"Not 'till we have an idea what happened here, Matthews. A shot can be heard a long way. Let me take a quick look around. I don't see any other bodies. Could be others down here."

Hiram remained in the saddle and watched as Joshua rode in a wide circle around the burnt out cabin and then into the brush. After a few minutes he re-appeared.

"I didn't see any other bodies. I did see some tracks over there," Joshua pointed. "Looks like about twenty riders, maybe more. Looks like they came from that direction and rode out west, northwest. The horses are unshod."

"Indians!" Hiram asked.

"Looks that way," Joshua replied.

The two men were about to dismount when they heard a woman's voice coming from their right. They turned in the direction of the voice just as a woman emerged from the brush. She was running in their direction. Her clothing was torn and she was smeared with blood and dirt.

"I knew you would come back, Albert," she spoke in German again. "I knew you wouldn't leave me."

The two men dismounted as she came quickly to them and collapsed into Hiram's arms. She got a closer look at Joshua and began to scream.

"Don't let them hurt me any more, Albert. Don't let them hurt me."

Hiram held the woman and tried to comfort her.

"What's she sayin' Matthews?" Joshua asked.

"I can't tell. Sounds like German. She seems to be afraid of you. I think you are right. Must have been Indians that hit these folks. I expect that body out there is her husband. This woman is out of her head."

It was obvious to Hiram that the woman had been severely treated. She continued to cling to him. He was able to push her back enough to see her face.

"Do you speak English?" he asked her.

She stared blankly at him and tried to bury her face in his chest again. Hiram tilted his head so he could speak to her and asked again. She clung to him whimpering.

"I don't think she's understanding you, Matthews. You want to keep trying, I'll run those buzzards off and see if there's anything left to bury."

Hiram lifted the woman's head from his chest. "Can you tell me your name?" he asked her. "Do you understand English?"

The woman was still unresponsive and looked at him through her crazed eyes. He gently brushed back the hair from her face. "Can you tell me who you are?" he asked again. "I want you to come with me," he told her. "I'm going to set you down over there in the shade. We're not going to hurt you. My name is Hiram. Do you understand what I'm saying to you?" he asked her as he gently guided her to a large rock under a big oak. The woman still did not respond.

Joshua walked back to Hiram and the woman. "Not much left to bury. I'll see if I can find a shovel. She say anything else yet?" he asked

"Not a word," Hiram responded. "She's scared out of her mind. She's been roughly treated."

"So what do ya want to do now?"

"I guess we'll have to camp here tonight if it's safe. I'll try to see if I can tidy this poor girl up some. I think it would be good if we could get some food in her. After that, I don't know. I can't go back to Fort Graham. Not again."

"I'll take care of the man then," Joshua said as he walked away.

Hiram had washed the woman's face and wrapped her in a blanket. Each time he tried to move from her side she became fearful and tried to cling to him. He was finally able to get her laid down on a bedroll as he sat next to her stroking her face and head. She finally lapsed into sleep. His thoughts turned to Sarah. He was thankful that when Ethan had been taken, she had been spared what had befallen the poor young woman who lay on his bedroll.

Joshua did what he could with the body of the man. He returned to Hiram and the woman. "Just to be on the safe side I'll take a better look around, Matthews. I want to make sure that those tracks don't double back this way. Maybe I can rustle up something for a meal. If she wakes up, you may want to move back into the brush till I get back. Make yourself a little less visible."

"I'll move her if I can, Joshua. You watch yourself," Hiram responded and returned to his vigil over the young woman.

After several hours Joshua returned. A fat rabbit dangled from his saddle horn. Hiram had seen him riding up. "Over here Joshua," he called out.

"I found some wild onions and good roots by a small creek a ways from here. Thought a good stew might be best for the woman. I followed the tracks for a good distance. They turned more west, but they aren't headed back here. We're safe enough for now."

"Then we'll stay here for the night like we planned. The woman may sleep through most of the night. Let's get that stew cooking and we can talk about what to do," Hiram replied. "Don't know that we have many options."

The young woman had slept through much of the night. Hiram was able to coax her to take a bit of the stew and some coffee. She was still sleeping, and he and Joshua sat drinking coffee discussing what to do. "Joshua, it's a given we can take this woman back to Fort Graham. That's another back track and another weeks' delay. I really have no desire to do that, but I don't know when we may run into another settlement or town this side of Fort Worth. I don't fancy being responsible for this young woman any longer than needed."

"We can make do on provisions. I just hope we don't run out of coffee. Maybe we can limit that to mornings," Joshua replied. "If Walker's map was right, I think we could push more due north from where we are and maybe hit Fort Worth in only another three or four days. Should be plenty of help up there."

"Then we push on," Hiram agreed. "But it's risky business. We could miss Fort Worth by fifty miles.

"Walker said it was a sizable town," Joshua observed. "According to him it's on the Trinity River. There's bound to be wagon trails going in and out. We have to cross the Brazos again, and then we should hit the Trinity north of there. There's bound to be settlers along the Trinity. The Wichita is somewhere north of there."

"Then let's get packed up and head toward Fort Worth."

Chapter Eighteen

Hiram rode double with the woman. She was too unhinged to trust her on a mount by herself. She remained silent at times. She cried out in German at times to her husband. Joshua rode a short distance ahead keeping his eyes open for any sign of trouble. They had turned due north as planned. He knew it would be a long ride to Fort Worth with the woman in such bad condition. He secretly hoped to find another small settlement with folks willing to look after her. They had ridden only a few hours when Joshua returned to their side.

"We're in luck," he informed Hiram. "I pushed out a bit ahead. There is a group of families about two miles ahead. Looks like another bunch of farmers. I think we should take this woman there. I didn't go near them. If they've had Comanche trouble, I didn't want 'em blowing my head off."

"I think it best we ride together from here then," Hiram replied. "When we get there, might be best you hang back out of sight until I see who they are and have time to introduce myself."

They rode in silence until they neared the camp. Hiram pulled up about a hundred yards out. "I'll give you a yell once I see that everything is all right. I don't want to spook these folks, whoever they are."

Hiram rode cautiously into the small compound. As he approached the woman grew more alert and agitated. He could see that there were men and women moving about in the compound. The woman suddenly began shouting out to the people. She was speaking German again and was struggling, trying to dismount. Two of the men looked up and came running toward Hiram and the woman. They were shouting in German. Hiram reined his mount to a stop as the men reached him. A young man reached up and grabbed the woman as she almost fell from the saddle.

"I'm Hiram Matthews," he said rather loudly. "I found this young woman a way back up the trail." He waited to see if anyone understood him. "Does anyone here speak English?" he asked.

"Yes, we speak the English," one man replied in a thick German accent. "What did you do to her?" another man asked.

"Whoa. Hold on a minute," Hiram replied. "My friend and I came across a burned out cabin a few miles from here. We found this young woman there."

"What happened to her?" the man asked.

"We found her like this." He paused and cocked his head to one side as if a revelation had occurred to him. "Do you know this young woman?" he asked, already suspecting the answer.

"Yes," the man answered. "She and her husband were part of our group. Where is Albert?"

"I think it best you tend to her. We shouldn't discuss this in her presence," Hiram replied.

Several of the women in the group had reached them. They took charge of the young woman and led her toward one of the small cabins. She was still incoherent.

"Is Albert her husband's name?"

"Yes. And her name is Katrin. Where is Albert?"

"She was speaking in German when we found her. She was out of her head. I don't speak German, but I do recall that she said the name Albert."

"Yes, Yes." the man interjected.

"But we also found a man's body. I assume it was him. Why she was left alive is a mystery."

"Albert is dead?" the man said quizzically. "How can this be?"

"The signs indicated that they were attacked by Indians," Hiram replied.

"But we were told that there have not been Indians in this area for many years," the man said. "Are you sure?"

"Well sir, my friend is convinced of it."

He remembered Joshua. He walked to a spot where he hoped Joshua could see him and whistled loudly and waived his hat over his head.

"You and your group may have suffered the same fate had this bunch not turned west. They're a bad lot, whoever they are. I doubt you have the ability to withstand such a bunch. How many people in your settlement?"

"We are four families. There are seven children." the man replied. "Are we in danger?"

"There is no way to be sure. This bunch could come riding back through here. If they do, I would not want to be in their path," Hiram replied." He turned to see Joshua was just riding up.

"This is my friend Joshua. We're heading north up to Fort Worth. I know it's a hard thing to think of, but you and your families may want to pull out with us. It will probably take about three or four days by wagon. We can notify the rangers when we get there. May be they or the army could dispatch some troops for a while."

"To think of such a thing we could not. We must be preparing our fields for planting. If we cannot make crops this year, we will not last until next spring."

"I know it's a hard thing to consider, but I encourage you to discuss it among yourselves. You're taking a big chance staying here with this bunch on the loose." Hiram encouraged the man.

"You and your friend should come with us please to the house. We will call everyone together," the man replied.

The group of settlers listened silently as their leader explained the situation. When he finished, the group began to discuss the matter. They spoke in German. At length the discussion was halted and the leader turned to Hiram.

"The women, they want to leave. They are fearful of these things you have told us. My friends and I feel we must stay. Do you think these bad people, they will come back?"

Hiram considered the question for a moment. "There is no way for me to know. It is possible. As I told you, their tracks took a more westerly direction. But if they were to return and they find you here, you and your families will be in grave peril."

The leader once again addressed his friends. There was more discussion, only this time more heated. After several minutes the leader again turned to Hiram.

"Will you take only our women and children to this Fort Worth with you?"

Hiram gave Joshua a glance. He turned back to the leader. "Look Mr....." he paused, "I don't believe I got your name."

"Alfred Schlemmer," the man replied and stuck out a hand." He then introduced the remainder of the group.

"Mr. Schlemmer I appreciate the pickle you're in. I do. But we're hardly prepared to be responsible for women and children. You're asking a great deal of us."

"The women, they can all handle a team and wagon. They would be to you no trouble. You said it is only maybe three or four days to this Fort Worth. If you take them there, they can come back with the soldiers."

"Mr. Schlemmer, there is no guarantee that there will be troops or rangers there. And Joshua and I can't lead them back here. We can give them general directions. I just don't know about all this."

"Matthews, do I get a say in all this?" Joshua interjected.

"Well, yes I suppose you do, but I think you and I should discuss it first. Outside," Hiram replied.

The two men left the cabin to discuss the matter. Joshua was the first to speak.

"This trail we're on, it's your's. I don't want to stick my nose where it don't belong. So, I won't say that we should or shouldn't do this thing. We could run into trouble ourselves, but it ain't likely. It's pretty sure these men won't go. If we leave the women and children here, and this bunch comes back, it's a bad thing. Taking them will cost us only a few days – if things go well. And I would hate to see anything bad happen to those kids. That's all I have to say."

Hiram was surprised by Joshua's thoughts on the matter. He stood silent for a long moment.

"If I can't talk Schlemmer and the others into coming with us, I suppose we have no other choice. But I will admit I'm a bit surprised at your willingness to do this."

"Told ya before I got a soft spot for crazy white fathers. I feel the same way about kids."

"Then let's get them packing. I'll speak to Schlemmer again. Maybe the men will change their minds. I can only hope that the women will not change theirs."

The following morning the wagons were packed and loaded. Tearful goodbyes were said and the passengers were loaded – five women and seven children.

"Schlemmer, I wish you and your friends would change your minds."

"Mr. Matthews, for your concern we thank you. With God's help, I am sure we will be all right. We must stay or we risk losing our land and all that we have built. To go we cannot."

Joshua had been silent all morning. He finally spoke.

"Mr. Schlemmer, it's best you keep a cold camp as much as possible. If you have fire, keep it to a minimum and use good dry oak to keep the smoke down. A good scout can smell smoke a mile away. Keep one man on lookout day and night. If that bunch comes back this way, you don't want to make it easy for them to find you."

"We are thankful for what you are doing and we will follow your advice. We will pray that God watches over you and our families."

Hiram and Joshua shook hands with the men and headed the precious cargo and wagons north.

Chapter Nineteen

Moving the wagons through the thickets and brush proved to be slow. Joshua rode a scout position ahead of the company, and Hiram rode at the lead. Progress continued through the day and at late evening, Joshua turned back to the group.

"There's a good clearing just ahead with a small creek close by. Looks like a good spot to settle for the day," he reported.

"How much ground do you think we covered today?" Hiram asked.

"Hard to say, Matthews what with all the maneuvering we had to do, but I expect we covered maybe six or eight miles is all."

"If we stay at this pace that means maybe four more days to Fort Worth, provided we don't miss it altogether."

Hiram halted the group in the clearing and instructed the women to prepare for the night.

"I think we have to run a cold camp tonight, Matthews. Don't want to send out invitations," Joshua suggested.

"I'll tell the women," Hiram replied.

Frieda seemed to be the matron of the women. She appeared to be the eldest, spoke fair English, and gave the orders. The others spoke and understood a little. Elissa tended the children. Anga and Hanna were the worker bees. They proved to be experienced with the teams and wagons. The children had tired of the wagons and were anxious to play. Bedtime came early for the children and the women. Katrin's condition had not greatly improved, but she had grown silent and more confused. After everyone was tucked away inside and under the wagons, Frieda came and sat beside Hiram and Joshua.

"I am sorry to you for these troubles. Our husbands, do you think will be safe?"

"Yes Ma'am, I believe they will be," Hiram assured her although he had his doubts. "Bringing you north with us is just the safest thing to do. With luck there will be troops available in Fort Worth to bring you back to your husbands. The bunch that hurt your friends are probably miles from here by now."

"We are thanking you for your help. Maybe tomorrow we will be making a fire and we will cook for you a good meal."

"That would be a relief," Joshua piped in. "Matthews ain't much of a cook. Jerky is his specialty. And his coffee ain't so hot either. Do you cook rabbit?"

"Rabbit, Squirrel, possum, turkey. You bring it. I will cook it. And it will be good."

The next evening the group dined on a small deer that Joshua had taken.

"That's as fine a meal as I've had in a long time," Hiram told the women.

"We will have meat for the trail also," Frieda added. "Tomorrow we will make the stew."

One of the little girls, Anya, had been eying Joshua all evening. He was aware that she had been watching him.

He crooked a finger and motioned her to come and sit next to him. To his surprise the little girl crawled up into his lap. She reached up and touched the feather that was woven into his long, black hair and spoke in German. Joshua responded in his Wichita language. The strange conversation continued for several minutes. It was as though they were actually understanding one another. The little girl continued to examine Joshua's hair and face with her tiny hands. Presently he reached back and took the feather from his hair and began placing it into the girl's hair. She smiled a broad smile, leaned in and kissed him on the cheek. Anya had made a conquest.

On the third day the brush and thicket began to disappear. The group soon found themselves traveling over a vast rolling prairie and their progress was much better. Joshua had scouted ahead and at midday he returned to report that he had picked up what appeared to be a trail heading northeast across the prairie.

"It's not much of a trail," he reported, "but my guess is, we follow it, we find Fort Worth."

"It's a good stroke of luck if it does," Hiram replied. The two continued to ride together for a while.

"That little girl last night. The two of you acted like you understood every word that was being said."

"We did, Matthews. She told me she liked my hair and the feather. Told her I liked her smile."

"Well, I know you're japing me, but danged if I don't believe it," Hiram replied and grinned.

Joshua became quiet and deep in thought for a while.

"You ever hunt buffalo, Matthews?" Joshua asked.

"Too busy chasing cows," he replied.

"They say a man could stand in one spot all day as the big herds passed by and not see the end of 'em. But now the buffalo are nearly gone. There are some way west and north. White hunters killing 'em all for their hides. I've been told that hunters can shoot as many as two or three hundred animals in a day. Skinners follow along in their wagons pulling the hides off with teams of mules. Leave the whole carcass laying to rot. It's destroyed the Indian way of life. I wish I had seen one of those big herds just once."

"I'll never understand the sort of greed that drives men to do such a thing," Hiram replied. "It's no wonder the native people hate white men."

"Don't forget Matthews, I'm one of those native people; at least partly."

"Do you hate white men?"

"Mostly," Joshua replied. "I make an exception now and then." He grinned.

"I'm glad you do, Joshua. Awfully glad you do."

Chapter Twenty

On the morning of the fourth day the trail came to what they assumed was the Trinity. It turned east along the river. That afternoon they sat on a high bluff on the south side of the river looking at Fort Worth in the distance.

"How the devil do we get these wagons across the river?" Hiram asked Joshua.

"Bound to be a crossing somewhere. You want to stay here and make camp; I'll follow the trail a bit to see if it leads to anything. We can cross tomorrow if I find a place."

Hiram was satisfied with the plan and Joshua rode off following the trail while Hiram prepared the women to make camp. Joshua returned just before sundown.

"There's a ferry downstream. I didn't go down all the way. Looked like it might take a wagon without the team."

The next day the group rolled into Fort Worth. They had not been prepared for what they found. They expected to find an army post. They were soon disappointed. The post had been abandoned some years earlier but the physical fort structure and a sizable community remained. Hiram made a few inquiries and found that there were troops at forts along the frontier. There were rangers in and out of Fort Worth and a small standing militia.

"We'll need to park these wagons somewhere while I see if I can find a local lawman. Maybe they can find some help for these women," Hiram instructed. "You get them situated and I'll find you."

Hiram stopped the first citizen he saw and inquired where to find the local sheriff or lawman.

"You'll find the local sheriff down Main Street," the man told him and pointed.

Hiram found the office and entered. After introductions and explanations the sheriff was of limited help.

"It's worry-some that Indians are making raids that far inside the frontier. I've heard rumors that Comanche activity has increased. I expect a town our size is safe. But the war is taking a toll on Texas. Aren't many troops available. Cattle prices are down to three, four dollars a head. Things are a mess. A lot of people have already left Fort Worth and we're short on men. We do have a small militia for any major threats. But they will be of no help to you. We've had no Indian problems here for some time so the rangers come through here only occasionally. I don't believe there are any in town right now."

"I've got a real problem here sheriff. I can't take these women and children with me and I can hardly leave them here unless I know somewhat of their fate."

"Well sir, what I can do is to notify the rangers next time any are through here. They may have information about any raids taking place. They may know when it's safe for these women to return to their farms, provided there's anything to return to. I can try to dispatch a man over to Dallas to see if there's any help available. Might be a patrol through here as well."

"I don't know how these folks will survive until then but I suppose I have to leave that part to them. I appreciate anything you can do for them.'"

"If you're planning on heading north you could be riding into trouble. Why not stay here until the rangers come through."

"I've other business up around the Wichita and Pease. But I would appreciate anything you can tell me about what lies ahead. I've never been in this part of the country."

The sheriff supplied Hiram with information and some general directions. The men shook hands and Hiram set out to find Joshua.

He found the group at the far end of town. He pulled Frieda aside and she listened intently as he explained the situation. When Hiram had finished explaining things she pulled herself erect and drew a deep breath.

"You should not worry for us. You have done so much already. We will be fine here. The wagons we have and the teams. God has led us this far and He will provide. The soldiers, they will come. You will see."

Hiram handed the woman some folded bills. "I wish I could do more," he told her.

She accepted the money only after some coaxing. "You and Joshua will stay tonight with us?" she asked.

"Yes. We will be off in the morning."

"Then we fix you a fine meal tonight," she replied and patted his shoulder.

Chapter Twenty One

They followed the Trinity when they left Fort Worth. There had been numerous small farms and ranches along the way and they had stopped and inquired at each. The answer was always the same. There had been no one who had knowledge of any encounters with Comanche or who remembered any hostages being ransomed in many years.

It was late February when Joshua and Hiram left the ranch. It was now April and Hiram had gotten no word, no clue, and no indication of any white captives being returned. There was no encouragement or hope being offered. Hiram had fought the feelings of hopelessness. He told himself over and over again that someone had seen his son – maybe living among the Comanches; that somewhere there was a clue, a rumor; that someone would remember a white child being returned or ransomed. But Hiram was beginning to lose his resolve. The only thing that kept him going was the hope that he and Joshua would find the friendly Comanche bands on the Pease and that by some miracle, some quirk of fate, his son would be found there.

They rode for days without seeing another settler, ranch, or farm. Joshua was now accustomed to riding out to scout what lay ahead. They were nearing the head waters of the Trinity.

Hiram was deep in thought as he rode. Joshua came galloping to his side.

"There's another ranch ahead, maybe a mile or so. Looks like a pretty big place. Barns and corrals. Maybe been there a while," he reported.

Joshua had come to respect Hiram as much as anyone he had ever known. He knew that Hiram was discouraged. He had grown less talkative in the past week. Joshua hoped that he would somehow play a part in seeing his friend reunited with his son. But he also knew in his own heart that it would take a miracle.

"Maybe this God that Matthews believes watches over men; maybe he'll grant Matthews his power. Maybe Matthews will receive a vision when he has his power," Joshua had thought. "Maybe I'll ask this God to help Matthews."

They rode in silence to the ranch. It was the same scene repeated again. Hiram had told the story to the rancher and his wife as he had done numerous times. When he had explained the quest, he sat back and looked intently at the rancher.

John Packston and his wife, Naomi were fine people. They had welcomed both men into their home without batting an eye. There had been no distinction made between Hiram and Joshua. They had come to the area almost twenty years earlier. They, like Hiram, had fought to build their ranch. Like he, they had faced every obstacle imaginable. There had been encounters with both friendly and unfriendly Comanches. They had buried two sons. So when Hiram told his story their hearts had been touched.

John studied Hiram's face for a moment. He looked at his wife's face. He could see the compassion in her eyes. He could see the desperation in Hiram's.

"Mr. Matthews, I've talked with people when they lost a loved one. I've seen and felt their grief. I've shared their grief, and I've shed tears with some of them. We buried our own two sons here on this place. Naomi and I have had our share of grief. I can see that you are still carrying a lot of it about your son, but you still have hope. I would not want to be the man that killed that hope. Neither would I want to give you false hope. So what I tell you now, I tell you with care."

"There have been two instances that I know of concerning hostage turnovers. I was involved in both. The Comanches up here sometimes trade for hostages with other Comanches. They then trade or sell the captives back to their families or anyone willing to pay their price. Both instances in which I was involved were within the time frame that makes them a possibility. Based on what you've told me, I don't believe your son was among those hostages."

Hiram broke in, "Well, at least what you are saying about the Comanches buying and selling hostages agrees with what I had been told. I guess I just had hoped that you might be the one."

"There's a bit more you need to hear, Mr. Matthews. At the last meeting about four, maybe five years ago the hostages were girls. They were bought back by a man and wife who had no children. I remember thinking what good folks they were. But that's not all I remember about the meeting. There were Comanche families there – men, women, children. I remember there was a boy - the age would have been about right - with one of the Comanche families. That is certainly nothing unusual. A Comanche family having a boy with reddish brown hair, well, that is. It stuck with me because it was so out of place. Either that child had a white father – which is not likely – or he was white."

Hiram could scarcely believe his ears. This good man had just offered him new hope. He found himself speechless. "Maybe I'm dreaming," he thought. "Did I really just hear what I thought I heard?" Before he could speak John continued.

"I told you I would hate to be the man to give you false hope. False hope is a cruel thing. So, please take what I've told you and measure it against reason. Don't convince yourself, against reason, that this was your son. It's a possibility at best. Nothing more."

"Mr. Packston, I knew when I set out on this trail that the idea of finding my son alive was an unlikely thing. I could never explain this feeling that he's out there somewhere. Maybe that's nothing more than false hope. But it's all I've got. So, yes Sir, I'll take what you've told me in the spirit it was given. You have my word on that. But true or false, win or lose, I am in your debt."

Naomi Packston was the next to speak. "Mr. Matthews, Joshua, You men have been on the trail a while. I believe a few days one way or another will not greatly change things. So I insist that the two of you spend a few days with us. Rest up some. Eat some good, nutritious food. There's room here for the both of you, and it would be our great pleasure to have you as our company for a few days. Please tell me that you will do this."

Hiram looked at Joshua and he nodded positively.

"I could use a bath and a good cleaning up. Yes Ma'am, we'll stay a few days."

The two enjoyed the Paxton's company for several days. Naomi Paxton was a loving and generous woman, and a good cook. She had spent some time with Joshua and had already grown fond of him and him of her. Hiram had not realized just how weary he had been. All things combined had taken a toll on him. He spent some time talking with John and found that it was likely that the Comanche family of whom they had spoken had moved off toward the north. After the few days' rest he was anxious to get back on the trail. He and Joshua had re-packed, and thanks to John and Naomi's generosity they had re-stocked for their continued journey. The time for goodbyes had come.

"John. Naomi. There's no way we can repay you for your kindness," Hiram said.

"I only hope you find what you're searching for, Hiram." John replied.

"When the time comes to return home Hiram I hope you and Joshua will find your way back here," Naomi told the men through tear filled eyes. "You will always be welcome here." She hugged both men. Joshua was a bit surprised and unaccustomed to that sort of affection.

"Mrs. Paxton, you've been really nice. You folks made me feel at home here." Joshua told Naomi.

The couple stood and watched as the two men rode away to the west.

After a short distance Joshua spoke. "Mrs. Paxton is a good person, Matthews. Makes me realize people ain't bad just because of their skin color. There's good people in all colors." He was silent for a minute. "This white God," he paused, "I think His power is strong, Matthews."

Chapter Twenty Two

Second Lieutenant Charles Williams served in the federal army until the outbreak of the war. When the Confederacy took over the forts in Texas, he resigned and joined the Confederacy. He had spent his early childhood in Alabama and had moved to Texas with his family after it's annexation into the union. His father was an army man and his father before him. Captain Trevor Williams had been sent to Texas during the Mexican American War and had distinguished himself as an officer and a leader. He was given a small command on the western frontier of Texas after the war. He had preached service to country to Charles and had shipped him off to The Virginia Military Institute when he turned seventeen. Upon graduation Charles had requested an assignment in Texas. He was granted his wish and was sent to Fort Chadborne. After four years of service he had seen action in several skirmishes with both Comanches and Kiowas. He had been the benefactor of the skill and knowledge of a seasoned, career military Sargent. Under Sargent O'Doherty's tutelage the young officer had learned what it meant to be an officer and a skilled commander. His current assignment was Fort Belknap on the north western frontier of Texas.

The now, First Lieutenant Williams was in charge of the patrol between Fort Belknap and Fort Brekenridge to the south. Belknap was one of a series of fortifications that the Confederates had manned to protect the western frontier. To the south of Belknap there was Brekenridge, Salmon and Pecan. To the north there was Cureton and Red River Station on the border. The Confederacy had taken over all federal forts when the war began and only Cooper to the west remained under federal control. Under Confederate control, the camps had been instructed to conduct patrols to their southern counterparts on a once a week basis. Each patrol was to consist of an officer and not less than ten troops. It was hoped that the regular show of force and movement would discourage Indian incursion into the frontier. The distances proved too great and allowed no time for actual scouting missions. It had become easy for raiders like Nocona and his band to slip in and out through the defenses.

On this particular morning, Lieutenant Williams lead his small platoon out on the patrol just like he had done for the past six months.

"Sergeant, I want one man on each flank of the patrol about a half mile out. Have them report back in every hour," he commanded Sergeant Graves.

"Yes sir. Will we be takin' the same trail as last week sir?" came the reply.

"That's correct Sergeant," he said. "And the week before that and the week before that," he thought to himself. His patrol of twelve men had been taking the same path every week for nearly six months. It had been the same each time. No problems, no Indian sightings, no anything except the same scenery. In spite of that fact the lieutenant was normally ever vigilant. There had been Indian incursions up and down the frontier since the war began, but never between Belknap and Brekenridge.

The patrol had ridden half the day with no event. They were nearing the crest of a small rise where the trail descended into a long draw with a steep, rocky, overhanging wall on their right and a densely wooded slope on the left.

Sergeant Graves reined his mount alongside the lieutenant as they approached the area.

"Any word from our flank riders, Sergeant?"

"Nothing to report sir."

"When did they last report?"

"Almost an hour, sir. They're due any time now."

"Very well, carry on Sergeant," Williams replied.

The patrol continued into the area. Midway through, the raiding party attacked. The flank riders had both been silenced with bow and arrow. The patrol was taken completely by surprise. Nocona had stationed some of his warriors along the top of the ridge on the right of the troops and more in the deep woods directly across. He had stationed a reserve at the end of the area to cut off any forward retreat and a smaller reserve to cut off any retreat to the rear. The troops would be caught in a cross fire with nowhere to go.

The first volley of fire knocked two riders from the saddle. Lieutenant Williams reacted immediately.

His immediate instinct was to ride through the ambush.

"Forward, forward," he shouted as he spurred his own mount.

A round caught his shoulder and he was nearly knocked from his mount. He continued to charge straight ahead with his remaining command. They were met with rifle fire at the end of the draw. Sergeant Graves was felled. Williams quickly evaluated the situation and quickly scanned for cover.

He wheeled his mount around and shouted for his men to make a dash for a small rock outcropping at the base of the cliff. His instincts were good and the close proximity to the face of the cliff would cut off the fire from above. Williams grabbed the saddle bags and canteen from his mount, and he and the remaining men jumped from their horses and flung themselves behind the rocks. He could see that Sergeant Graves was trying to move to the cover of an old tree trunk near to where he had fallen. Bullets continued to ping off of the rocks. The eminent danger was coming from the deeply wooded area directly to his front. His troops were firing wildly into the woods. He realized that they would have no chance of survival unless they rationed their resources. He checked Sergeant Graves again. He had made the cover of the fallen tree and Williams decided that he was safe for the moment.

"Cease fire. Cease fire," he yelled as loudly as he could. His troops were surprised by the command, but they trusted his instincts and stopped firing.

"No one takes a shot unless they have a well-defined target," he commanded. "Check your ammo supply. Did any of you grab water or ammo?"

"Grabbed my canteen and some ammo, sir," one of the men reported.

"Anyone else?" Williams asked. None of the others had held the presence of mind to grab either. "Then we have the private's extra ammunition and the ammunition from my bags and two canteens. I want one gun on Sergeant Graves at all times. Corporal, please make sure that happens. Ration the water and bullets. Our best strategy is to hold our position and wait. We have no idea how large an opposition force we are facing. If we can hold out through the night, the fort will send out a search party."

With the rush of adrenalin, he scarcely realized he had been wounded. The corporal low crawled to the lieutenant's side.

"Sir, you're bleeding from your shoulder. You better let me take a look at that."

"I believe the bullet shattered my shoulder Corporal. I can't move my arm. You'll have to cut the sleeve away. See if you can get the bleeding stopped."

The corporal confirmed what the lieutenant had told him. "Sir, I need to put pressure on that wound for a while. It's bleeding some, but not all that badly right now. Sir, what's our chances if this bunch tries to rush us?"

"I doubt that will happen, Corporal," Williams replied. "Based on our casualties, I don't believe there are more than a couple of dozen or so out there. If there were many more, I doubt any of us would have survived. We just need to remain calm and patient. That search party will be sent out tomorrow."

Williams was calculating in his head when help could be expected. By his calculation it would be noon the next day at best.

Chapter Twenty Three

Hiram and Joshua left the Packston ranch headed west toward Fort Belknap. It was no more than two days ride according to John Packston. John had suggested that they stop at the fort. They could then swing down to Brekenridge and then west to Cooper. They rode together and talked as they rode.

"By my reckoning we should be within no more than twenty miles of Belknap, Joshua. If we push it I think we could make it today."

Joshua was rested and feeling good.

"If you can make it, old man, I can make it," he jabbed at Hiram.

"Who you calling old man, smart Alec? I'm not even eighty yet," Hiram jabbed back and kicked his mount up to a slow trot. Joshua kicked his mount and caught up with Hiram.

"Now I'm more worried about your mount making it Matthews, carrying all that weight from Mrs. Packston's cooking. The way you were gobbling it up they were probably glad to see us go," he jabbed again.

"Keep it up and I'll take my horse back and make you walk," Hiram retorted.

The two continued at a slow trot for a while. Joshua suddenly reined his mount to a stop. Hiram looked back to see what was happening and turned his mount back to Joshua.

"Something wrong with your mount, Joshua?"

"I'm sure I hear gun shots, Matthews."

The two men sat, listening intently.

"There. Did you hear that?"

"That's definitely gun fire. But that's a long way off, Joshua. Could be military maneuvers, but the fort's still fifteen or twenty miles."

"Do we check it out?" Joshua asked. "We could be riding into the middle of something."

"I think we have to see what's going on considering what we ran into with the German families back down the trail. I don't fancy riding into what's going on like we're the cavalry so let's take a little time and go in slow. How far away do you think those shots were?"

"As faint as it was, I'd say more than a mile – that way," Joshua said and pointed.

They kicked their horses and sped off in the direction of the last reports.

Joshua held up his hand and they reigned in their mounts.

"We leave the pack horses and go slow from here," he said. They could hear the report of sporadic rifle fire. They were close. They continued to close in on the shots.

"Whatever's going on is just over that rise, Matthews. I think we go on foot from here."

Chapter Twenty Four

Nocona had not counted on the young officer's calm when his patrol came under fire. He had envisioned the troops fleeing forward into his rifles and being turned back into the rifle fire at their rear. The fire from the rear was supposed to turn the troops back into the fire from the front. All of this time the warriors on the top of the canyon wall and across from the wall would rain down fire from above. He had not counted on the troops being able to take cover that would block the fire from above. He had made a strategic mistake, but his warriors had the troops pinned down. It was now all about time. Nocona knew that when a patrol did not report in as expected other troops would be dispatched. He rode to the top of the canyon wall where his riflemen were stationed above the patrol on the strategic high ground. The troops were pinned down directly below but were protected from gunfire from above by the overhang of the canyon wall. Nocona swiftly moved his warriors who had lain in wait at the front and rear of the patrol. He moved them to the top of the canyon wall above the troops. The warriors across the draw kept the troops pinned down.

"Gather dry brush and green cedar brush," he commanded his warriors. "Throw it over the edge. We will drive them from the rocks with fire." The warriors began gathering the brush and tossing it over the small cliff.

"What are they doing sir?" the corporal asked Williams.

"My guess is they plan on burning or smoking us out. Have the men stay as close to the cliff face as possible. Help me move back."

Hiram and Joshua had crept to the top of the rise. They could see clearly what was going on and they saw the two fallen troops. They were about one hundred yards out. They could see about a dozen warriors working furiously throwing the brush over the wall.

"That bunch has those troops in a bad spot, Joshua. Looks like they plan on burning them out."

"Yeah, and that rifle fire coming from that heavily wooded area on the left has 'em pinned down. What do you suggest?"

"How good are you with that rifle?"

"Good enough, but maybe not from this range. Looks like to me we can get closer if we follow this brush line to our left."

"We're only two guns. We start shooting and they realize that, chances are some of 'em will come after us. But whatever we do, we better do it before they set fire to that brush."

The pile of brush had grown to a considerable size and was piled high just in front of the rocks directly in front of the troops.

"Looks like two of them are trying to get a fire going, Joshua. Let's get closer fast. Once we are in position, I think we can move fast up and down that brush line. If we fire quickly from different positions they may overestimate our numbers. Let's move."

The two men moved quickly along the brush line. They were soon in position.

"I'll take the two trying to get the fire going. You move to the left and I'll move right. With a little luck we may be able to spook them," Hiram instructed.

Hiram took dead aim on the two building the fire. His first shot missed. The raiders were surprised by the rifle fire and stood frozen just long enough for Hiram to get off another shot. The bullet found it's mark and the warrior fell with a bullet to the chest. Joshua began firing and moving along the brush line. He took aim on a second assailant. His shot found it's mark and the second warrior fell. The group began to scatter and Joshua was able to hit another man. Hiram moved and took another shot. He caught the second fire starter in the thigh. Another missed shot.

He moved and quickly adjusted his aim and took another shot. The two men continued to move and fire.

Shining Rocks was watching and saw that the fire was coming from several locations.

"There are more soldiers. They will kill us all," Shining Rocks yelled.

The second warrior lighting the fire had managed to get a small flame going before Hiram had wounded him. He struggled to his feet and picked up a burning branch. He began limping toward the edge of the cliff carrying the branch. Hiram took careful aim and squeezed the trigger. The warrior fell short of the edge.

Joshua was still moving up and down the brush line firing. Nocona signaled for his warriors to mount and retreat. The warriors in the brush line saw that Nocona and the others were retreating and they too sprinted to their horses. Joshua and Hiram continued to move and repeat fire as quickly as possible. Another warrior fell. The two kept up their firing until the raiders were out of range. They watched as the two groups of raiders joined and sped away.

"I believe our little bluff worked, Matthews."

"It looks that way. But let's get down there quick. That bunch may re-group and come back."

The two men sprinted to their mounts and raced toward where the troops had been trapped.

The corporal had left his covered position and greeted Joshua and Hiram.

"I don't know who you fellows are, but I'm damn glad to see you. That bunch had us cold."

"Glad we came along when we did," Hiram replied. "Do you have wounded?"

"Yes sir," the corporal replied. "Lieutenant Williams took one in the shoulder. He's been bleeding pretty bad and he's unconscious. Sergeant Graves is over there." He pointed. "Haven't gotten to him yet. Don't know if he's still alive."

"I'll take a look, Matthews," Joshua offered.

"We've got two dead, sir – that we know of. Maybe two more. Two flank men never reported in before they hit us."

"All right Corporal," Hiram said. "Let's pull things together pretty quickly. We need to get moving as quickly as possible. Don't want to be here if that bunch or another one like them comes riding in here."

"Yes sir," the corporal replied. He turned and began to bark orders at the remaining troops. Hiram rode over to Joshua and the Sergeant.

"He's wounded pretty bad, Matthews. He took a round through the right side of his chest."

"We need to see if we can find any of the troop mounts, Joshua. I'll have the corporal tend to this man. Can you find us some mounts?"

"I'll see what I can do."

"You watch yourself Joshua."

Hiram returned to the corporal.

"We will need to make two travoises to carry the lieutenant and the Sergeant. I've got my friend looking for mounts. Someone will need to tend to the Sergeant. How far to the nearest help?"

The corporal instructed two men to begin making the rigs to carry the wounded and two to tend to Sergeant Graves. "Closest help will be back at Belknap. What about our dead sir?"

"Corporal, I hate to say this, but we may have to leave them and send a party back from Belknap. We simply don't have time and if we don't have enough mounts we can't take them."

Joshua had been gone about thirty minutes. The troops had Williams and Graves loaded onto make shift travoises. Hiram had ridden back to pick up the two pack horses and was just back when Joshua returned. He had no mounts with him.

"Found one more dead up the trail a way. I can maybe find another mount or two, but it will take time. The gun fire spooked 'em pretty bad. I'm not crazy about riding around out there either."

"We've got four mounts including the two pack horses. The two wounded may not make it if we don't send them ahead. It will be slow going," Hiram assessed. "Corporal, how long do you think it will take for a single rider to get back here with help?"

"I can send Private Yates, sir. He's the best horseman we have. He can make the fort by first light. It will take a bit to get a patrol mounted. We'll run out of daylight in an hour or so. It's slow moving with a column at night, so I doubt they can move until morning anyway. My best guess is late tomorrow at best."

"All right then, Corporal," Hiram replied. He pondered the situation for a moment. "Send Yates right now. Get one of your men to unload the pack horses. Let him pick the best two mounts. The other two horses and riders can pull the wounded. They will need to move as quickly as possible. We'll have to leave the dead for now. The rest of us will have to go it on foot."

"I don't like splitting up like that, Matthews. If we send the two riders ahead with the wounded, what happens if they run into trouble?" Joshua responded.

"I know it's chancy, Joshua, but we need to get the wounded moving quickly."

Joshua did not respond. The corporal approached Hiram and Joshua.

"I'm staying behind to watch over our dead, sir. I'm the senior man in the group. It's only right I stay. I won't leave our men out here for the varmints."

"I don't advise it Corporal, but I understand. Let's move the dead behind the rocks and gather their weapons," Hiram replied. "Let's get this group moving."

Chapter Twenty Five

The Corporal was right. Yates was an accomplished horseman and he understood what a good horse could and could not do. Private Yates pushed his mount to the limit until dark. When it was no longer safe to keep his mount at a full gallop, he slackened his pace. He didn't want to have his first mount misstep in the dark and break a leg. It would be worse still if he were injured. He was acutely aware of what was riding on his swift return to the fort. His comrades' and his commander's life was dependent on him. He would keep the unmounted horse in reserve for the sprint to the fort.

Morning at the fort was a busy time. Troops were mustering for morning roll call. Lookouts and guards were being relieved and the cooks were readying for the morning meal. The forward lookout had been at his post only a few minutes when he spotted Private Yates.

"Single rider coming in and he's coming fast," he yelled to the watch commander, Lieutenant Helms.

"Can you identify?" Helms called back.

"He's uniformed, sir."

"Is he under pursuit?"

"Not that I can tell sir."

The Lieutenant ordered the gates to be opened. In only a minute the Private reined his mount to a hard stop in front of the watch commander and literally jumped from the saddle.

"Sir, our patrol was hit by hostiles yesterday. Four dead and two wounded," he reported breathlessly.

"Slow down Private. Is your patrol still under attack?" Helms asked.

"No sir. At least not when I was sent out to bring help."

"What is the estimated strength of the hostiles?"

"Sir, I don't know for sure. Lieutenant Williams didn't think it was a large force. I only saw about a dozen, maybe more."

The Lieutenant turned to his First Sergeant.

"Sergeant, begin preparations to mount a relief patrol of fifty men and three wagons. Have them ready to ride in fifteen minutes. Tell Doc he will need to come with us. Private, how far were you out when you were attacked?"

"Sir, we were about half way to Brekenridge," Yates replied.

"Is the patrol in danger of another imminent attack?"

"I don't believe so, sir. Sir, Mr. Matthews had the Corporal send the wounded out ahead and the rest are coming in on foot."

"Good god," the lieutenant replied. "They're out in the open and moving with hostiles in the area?"

"Yes sir. Mr. Matthews thought it was best to try to put more distance between them and the hostiles."

"Who in the devil is this Mr. Matthews, Private?"

"Sir, he and his friend came along when we were under attack. They're the reason the hostiles broke off."

"Tell me about it later then Private. You rode all night?"

"Yes, sir."

"Are you physically up to leading us to the location of the patrol?"

"Yes sir. If they stick to the trail we always take."

The Lieutenant quickly reported the situation to the fort commander and within the hour the relief patrol was moving.

Chapter Twenty Six

Nocona was furious over the failure of the attack. He had counted on having the additional rifles and ammunition that the troops carried. He had led his group away after they came under counter attack from Hiram and Joshua's rifles. He soon realized that his band was not being pursued by what he had estimated to be a larger mounted patrol. After only several miles, he halted his warrior band and dismounted.

"The white soldiers, they have not followed us," he told Shining Rocks. "I think they are not many. If they were they would follow us."

"We should return and fight the whites again."

"We will send scouts back to see if the white soldiers are many," Nocona said. "They will not travel at night. We will camp here and wait for our scouts."

The horses and men carrying the wounded soldiers had set a fast pace and were ahead of the men on foot. When the scouts caught up with the group on foot they had no way of knowing that. What they saw was a small group of men, and they were without mounts. Nocona would be glad to hear the report. They could still kill the soldiers and take their rifles. The scouts returned to the camp and reported what they had seen.

"How can this be? Why do they walk at night?" Nocona asked. "There were many rifles firing from the brush. You did not see them all in the dark. Maybe the soldiers that attacked us are following behind the ones who walk."

The scouts assured Nocona that they had thoroughly checked for other forces. "We speak the truth," they said. "We are sure that the men on foot are the only soldiers."

Nocona was still very puzzled how he could have been so mistaken. "If there are other soldiers, we will see them when the sun comes," he said. "The others will not move quickly without horses. They will be easy to kill."

Chapter Twenty Seven

Hiram, Joshua, and the soldiers had been pushing hard through the night, but their progress was slowed by the darkness. The soldiers knew the terrain and had been able to keep the group on track. They had been on foot for about six hours and were nearing exhaustion. Hiram was the oldest man in the group and it had been particularly hard for him.

"How far do you think we've come, Joshua?" he asked.

"A man can cover two miles an hour at best in this terrain," he replied. "How long we been walking, Matthews."

Hiram pulled a pocket watch from his jeans watch pocket. It was a gift given to him by Sarah some years before her death. "I'm not sure exactly when we started walking, but it's been five or six hours. That means we have probably come ten miles or so. I don't know how much longer we can keep up this pace, Joshua. I think we've got to stop for a while. These boots I'm wearing weren't designed for walking. These men need rest too."

"Then we should rest for a bit, Matthews. I'm spent too. I think we're safe enough for now. If that bunch was coming back they would have caught us by now. But Comanche don't mind riding at night."

Hiram signaled the group to stop and informed the troops. "Anyone disagrees, speak up. I guess I've sort of taken over here and you men don't have to take any orders from me."

"Look sir, if it wasn't for you and your Indian friend we would probably all be burned to death. You've gotten us this far, and I sure as heck don't have any objections following your lead." The other soldiers expressed their agreement.

"Then we will rest here a spell. I'm too tired to sleep. I'll stand watch for a while and I'll wake one of you when I need relief."

Hiram and Joshua sat and leaned against a tree.

"If we made ten miles and that patrol gets away at day break, they should meet up with us maybe late morning, Joshua. I think we're gonna make it."

"Didn't know you were such a take charge sort of guy, Matthews. Your thinking saved all these men's lives today. But I'm not convinced that bunch of raiders won't figure out that nobody's chasin' 'em. They figure that out, we still may have a fight on our hands. Those two horses pulling the wounded are leaving a trail that a kid could follow. I hope we're right about how far we've come and how quickly help gets here. That bunch hits us out here in the open, we're all dead men."

"I guess you didn't figure on all this excitement when you signed on back in Waco. This is the second time I've just about gotten you killed."

"Excitement? Is that what this is called, Matthews? Hell, I've been misinformed all this time thinkin' excitement was supposed to be fun."

"Well I guess I've had about all the fun I can take for one day," Hiram replied.

The two sat silent for a spell. Both were too keyed up for sleep.

"What month is this, Matthews?"

"I believe it's mid-April, Joshua. I've sort of lost track of time as of late. Why do you ask?"

"No particular reason. Just wondering if we're gonna be in the middle of the heat when we hit the Estacado."

"I expect it will be full spring by the time we get to the Pease. But winter may not be through. I've seen snow on the ground in March back home. We've been lucky with the weather so far but we'll be further north."

The men sat silent for a long moment. Hiram was thinking how he had come to consider Joshua a friend but he knew little about him.

"How is it that you scouted for the army and never made it north, Joshua?"

"Scouted mostly in the south. The war with the Mexicans was winding down but they still needed scouts down there. I wasn't much more than a kid. Always wanted to come north though. Wanted to see those buffalo. After the army let me go I thought about it. Just never got started after I went back to Waco. Had a wife with me. Thought we might raise a family but she died."

"Who taught you to speak English?"

"I was a kid in Waco, there was an old white man took a shine to me. I spent a lot of time with him. He was the only friend I had as a kid. Weren't any Indian kids around. White kids wouldn't have anything to do with me. That is other than to kick my ass when they got a chance. So I stayed away from 'em and spent time with that old man. He was good to me. Taught me good English. One of two white men I've made an exception for."

Hiram knew he was the other.

"Funny how things work out. I grew up in Missouri. Ended up in the army for a while when I was nothing more than a kid. Came to Texas to make a life. Seems like our lives ran sort of the same path for a while."

Joshua didn't reply. He was thinking about his wife and the family he never had. The two men lapsed back into silence.

Chapter Twenty Eight

Nocona commanded his men to mount up well before daylight. His plan was to send scouts out again in the light. They would see if there were additional troops following the troops on foot. "This could be a clever trap," he had thought. "Their main force could be following the troops on foot. They may hope to lure us in and then kill us with their rifles."

"We will chase the troops that are on foot," he told his men. "But we will not attack them until we know their numbers."

Hiram, Joshua and the group of soldiers had resumed their walk after a few hours of rest. They had moved about twelve miles north east of Nocona's band. The relief detachment had moved at a trot and was nearing the location of the men on mounts that were bringing in the wounded.

Joshua had moved ahead of the group and moved to the top of a small hill. He could see a fair distance in every direction. He looked back to the south west and studied the horizon. His eyes froze on what appeared to be a dust cloud not more than three miles out.

"Damn, I need glass," he said to himself and turned to hastily join the group. When he returned, the troops gathered near to hear his report.

"Matthews, I saw what I'm pretty sure was a dust cloud off to the south."

"Can't be the troops from Belknap. Private, any chance that's a column of troops out of Brekenridge?"

"I don't think so, Mr. Matthews. Scouting groups are instructed to move to forts to their south."

"If it's that bunch of fighters coming back they'll be close in half an hour. They pick up our trail right away and they could be on us in less than that, Matthews."

"If the troops left Belknap at daylight they've got to be close, Joshua. Do you think we should keep moving or try to find decent cover and wait?"

"If that bunch catches us in the open we're done. It's a big "if " counting on the troops from Belknap. I figure they would have had to cover fifteen miles or more since daylight to be anywhere close. I think our best chance is to find some cover on high ground and try to hold out until the troops come. There's not much cover on the hill I was just on, but it's the best high ground around."

"What do you men think?" Hiram asked the troops. They all expressed their agreement.

"Then let's get to that hill and see what kind of defense we can build," he replied.

Joshua was watching intently to the south. The troops had been able to drag a few fallen tree trunks to their position and had made some makeshift cover.

"There," Joshua said and pointed as Nocona's band came into the open from behind a densely wooded area. They were no more than a mile away. "If they have picked up our trail they'll be on us in no time."

Nocona's scouts had picked up the tracks made by the travoises. It had been easy to follow them to the group on foot. They had confirmed that the group was the entire troop force. The scouts returned and reported sighting the group of soldiers. They informed Nocona that they had taken defenses on a small hill. Now they were bearing down on the small group with a party of twenty warriors. Nocona halted his raiding party to make plans for the attack.

"It will be hard attacking them. The high ground gives them the advantage," he told Shining Rocks. "We have to split our forces and attack them from two directions." He took a stick and drew in the dirt. "We will send half of our warriors directly at them from here. You will go with these warriors. I will circle them and attack from behind here. I will not attack until they have trained their forces on you. We will surprise them. Tonight we will smoke and tell of how we killed the white soldiers."

Chapter Twenty Nine

The mounted troops pulling the wounded had moved well ahead of the group on foot. It was mid-morning when they were sighted by the relief patrol. Lieutenant Helms gave the order for the troop to advance at full gallop. He halted his troop when they met the troops pulling the wounded.

Doc was the first to dismount. He was not a doctor, but he was the best medic that Helms had ever known. He had served for a year on the battlefields back east before being shipped west. He had learned what he knew by firsthand experience in a few of the bloodiest battles ever fought. He hurriedly began checking the two wounded men.

"Graves is dead Lieutenant. Lieutenant Williams is serious. His shoulder is hit bad. I'll do what I can to help him but he needs a surgeon. That arm gets infected, if it's not already, he's going to lose it. I need to get him on a wagon and get him to the fort."

The lieutenant turned to his Sergeant. "Get the Lieutenant, Sergeant Graves and these two troops on to a wagon. Pick out ten men to escort them back to the fort." He turned his attention to the two who had brought in the wounded. "How far back do you estimate to the troops on foot?"

"Couldn't be more than two, three miles is all sir," one of the troops reported.

"Sergeant can we follow the travois tracks if we move at a gallop?" the Lieutenant asked.

"I believe we can sir," the Sergeant replied.

"Then let's get this troop moving." He mounted and gave the order.

Chapter Thirty

The troops, Hiram and Joshua had spread themselves in a circle behind their makeshift defense.

"This bunch could hit us from any direction." Hiram told his new command. Won't surprise me if they try hitting us from more than one direction. That's what I would do. Keep your eyes open."

Shining Rocks had moved his small force under the protection of cover to within several hundred yards of the troops. His group would make a false charge toward the hill to draw fire and train the troop's attention on him and his group. The plan was to charge only close enough to draw fire before they broke off. He had given Nocona ample time to ride in a wide circle and get in position on the opposite side of the little knoll. He was ready to begin the attack.

He gave the order and he and his group broke cover and rode directly at the hill. When the young troops saw the party they began firing immediately. Hiram had neglected to instruct the men to hold their fire until the raiders were within a good perimeter of fire. He had overestimated their experience. Shining Rocks and his warriors continued to charge the hill. At the first rifle report Nocona and his men had begun their charge. He hoped to catch the soldiers while they were reloading.

A half mile away Lieutenant Helms and his troops had also heard the report of the first rifle shot. He immediately ordered his troop to a full out pace.

Nocona's warriors mounted the attack from the rear just as Shining Rocks and his warriors broke off their charge. Nocona and his warriors were charging straight ahead up the hill and were within no more than two hundred feet from Hiram and the troops. Several of the men were reloading and Nocona was able to press the attack. When the soldiers began firing toward Nocona's warriors, Shining Rocks and his group had once again pressed the attack from the front. Hiram's troops were panicked and were firing wildly and hitting nothing. Nocona could smell victory.

The relief patrol had charged straight at the noise of the gun fire. Lieutenant Helms and his troops came charging around the base of the hill from Shining Rocks left. He and his warriors were caught totally by surprise. Before they could realize that they were under attack, five of his warriors were knocked from their mounts by the rifle fire of the charging troops. He and the rest of his men wheeled in a full retreat and two more were struck down. Shining Rocks' horse was hit and he was thrown head over heels into a broken heap. The other warriors sped away with troops hot on their heels.

Nocona saw from the other side of the hill what was happening and he wheeled his horse to retreat. His warriors followed suit. Hiram and his troops were still firing in Nocona's direction. He took careful aim at one of the retreating warriors. Nocona felt the bullet when it slammed into his spine at the base of his neck. It was the last sensation he would ever feel as he fell from his mount. The troops on top of the hill jumped to their feet and began shouting and jumping up and down. Two minutes earlier they were surely dead. Now they were alive and they could not contain their jubilation.

Chapter Thirty One

Lieutenant Helms rode to the top of the hill and dismounted.

"Looks like you were in a real bind here," he overstated the obvious.

"If you hadn't shown up when you did I'm afraid we were all done for Lieutenant," Hiram said as he extended his hand and introduced himself and Joshua.

"I'm Lieutenant Helms. I'm the watch commander out of Fort Belknap. Is this what's left of our patrol?"

"There are two dead back down the trail. One of your troops, a Corporal, is back there. He refused to leave the dead unattended. I believe he's all right."

"We will require a full report when we get you men to Belknap, but we've other business here first. You'll want to know that a few miles back we picked up the men you sent ahead with the wounded. Unfortunately, Sergeant Graves did not survive. He was a good man. I believe we owe you and your friend a debt of gratitude."

"I'd be satisfied with a meal and a cot Lieutenant. I'm bone weary and so are your troops. We covered a lot of ground."

"I can't say that I agree with that decision, but if you hadn't made it there is little doubt you would all be dead now."

"Do you know who this bunch was Lieutenant?"

"I'm afraid not Mr. Matthews. There are bands like this bunch on the loose up and down the frontier. But we've had no contact with hostiles until today. We will get you men loaded up and see if there are any survivors among their fallen. If you will excuse me, I'll tend to the clean-up."

Helms instructed his detail to check for survivors. A short while later he was informed that there was one man still alive but critically injured. Shining Rock's mount had been shot out from under him.

"This one is still alive," Doc reported. "His back is probably broken. I'm pretty sure he broke some ribs, and I believe the ribs may have punctured a lung. He's coughing up blood. He won't last long, Lieutenant. He's mumbling something in Comanche. Sounds like he keeps repeating a name – Nocona."

"Get Matthews and his Indian friend over here. The Indian may be able to understand him," Helms instructed.

Joshua knelt beside Shining Rocks and listened intently. "He's saying something about a witch. He thinks a witch put a curse on him. I can't make sense of it." He paused as if in thought and listened. "Nocona. He's saying Nocona, Matthews."

"We've heard of this Nocona, Lieutenant. A ranger back at Graham warned us about him. He said this Nocona was raiding the frontier. Said he was a dangerous man. I suspect we saw some of his work a while back. We ran across a burned out farm. There was a woman out of her mind. Her husband was dead."

"The woman, Matthews," Joshua interrupted. "They left her alive and we couldn't figure out why. My money says they thought she was a witch for some reason. Maybe because she was out of her head. Lots of Indians are superstitious about that sort of thing. That's what he's talkin' about. I'd bet on it."

"Then this man is not this Nocona fellow." Helms surmised. "Could be he escaped. There were a few that slipped through our hands. If he was their leader, at least we've put him out of business for a while. I guess it's no matter really. This is one bunch less for Texas to worry about."

Shining Rocks had stopped mumbling and was coughing up blood. He drew a shallow breath, closed his eyes, and joined his ancestors.

"Sergeant, send a party of ten men to find the Corporal and recover our dead. Take one of the wagons," Helms ordered.

"Organize another party to gather up the dead. We can lay them out but we lack the gear to bury them."

"Lieutenant, we had to leave all of our gear. We had to use our pack horses to bring in the wounded. I'd like to recover that. There are items in our gear that I can't replace."

"We'll find your gear Mr. Matthews. Tell the Sergeant where you left it and we'll make sure you get it back," Helms turned to the Sergeant. "Prepare the remainder of the detail to camp here tonight. We'll move at daylight tomorrow."

Chapter Thirty Two

The relief column rolled into Fort Belknap the following day. The fort commander had left word for Lieutenant Helms to report immediately upon arrival. Colonel Robert Savage had been in command at Belknap for only a year. His command had been involved in no confrontations with hostiles. He had served in the Union army prior to Texas joining the Confederacy and had been on track to become a general. His strong ties to the south had won out. He hoped that he would be sent east to join in the war effort there. But he was now stuck at Belknap, and his role had been reduced to protecting an almost indefensible frontier. He was anxious to hear the details of the incident that had taken place. Lieutenant Helms was told to report to the Colonel immediately. Helms asked Hiram to join him to make a full account. Introductions were made and Colonel Savage asked the Hiram to take a seat.

"Lieutenant, I assume you have invited Mr. Matthews to join us for a good reason."

"Yes sir. He has knowledge of the events that I do not possess. I felt it was important that they relate the incident."

"In that case, please proceed."

Hiram told the story of his and Joshua's role in the attack. He was careful to add as much detail as possible. The Colonel listened carefully as he described the incident.

"It is fortunate that you two came along when you did. It appears that our casualties would have been much higher had you not. The Confederacy is grateful for your courage and leadership. I am curious as to how it is that you just happened to be in this area."

"Colonel, we have personal business up on the Pease. Joshua and I are anxious to get under way again. In fact, if we can get our mounts and personal belongings, we would like to be moving tomorrow."

Colonel Savage sat for a moment in thought. "Mr. Matthews, you are heading into an area that has become increasingly unstable. This group that you encountered is probably one among any number of similar groups. They may even be part of a much larger contingency of hostiles. Comanche raids have increased in many areas and we are spread too thin. I am surprised that we haven't seen more contact in our area before now."

"Colonel, it was my understanding that most of the Comanches up on the Pease are not considered as hostiles."

"I'm afraid that you were misinformed. Before the war started that was largely true. I'm afraid that it has become increasingly difficult to know who's friendly and who isn't. I will tell you that many of the non-hostiles have moved off toward the Indian Territory onto reservation land. Even that is suspect. Reports are that some hostiles make their raids and retreat to the safety of the reservations. Are you indicating that you somehow have business with the Comanches?" the Colonel asked skeptically.

"Colonel, it's a long story but the short version is that I believe my son may have been taken by the Comanche and may be living among them in the area around the upper Pease."

"Mr. Matthews, it's my job to guard the citizens of Texas and to prevent interaction with hostiles when possible. Every time there is an incursion by whites into an active area it creates unrest. Then the army is forced to get involved. So you can see it's not just your safety that concerns me." He paused for a moment as he considered the situation. "How old is your son?"

"He will be almost thirteen now."

"Then he would be too young to ride with war parties as a fighter. If your son is living with the Comanche it is highly possible that he could be among the non-hostiles in Indian Territory." Savage paused and considered what to say next. "The patrol from Red River station is due in here tomorrow and they will be returning the day after. They can provide you with safe passage to the border near Indian Territory. It seems logical to me that you continue your search there." He searched Hiram's face for any indication that his suggestion was meeting with acceptance. "I'd like you to consider this possibility. But if you are determined to search around the Pease, I suggest that you start at Fort Cooper. There are Union troops there. It may be they can assist you and I believe you would be safe getting to Cooper. But for now, I'd like to hear more about your son, Mr. Matthews," the Colonel requested.

Hiram shared the full story with the Colonel including what had been shared with him by Mr. Paxton. He summed up his story by agreeing with the Colonel. "When Mr. Paxton saw the boy he was with non-hostiles. Maybe you're right Colonel. I think we'll take your advice and head on up to the territory. Besides, I don't think Joshua and I savor the idea of running into another party like Nocona's bunch."

"I understand your desire to continue your search, Mr. Matthews. I do. I wish you God speed in your journey. I will do what I can to help you once you arrive at Red River Station. I have some contacts there, and I will send a letter to the Commander up there. It may be that he can supply you with information and put you in contact with the right agent," the Colonel offered. "I met an agent named Holmes several years ago, and I believe that he may be of help. Now, we must get you and your friend settled in for the time being. I still want to meet him and give him my thanks. I'll have the First Sergeant take you to quarters. You'll find our cooks here provide a very fine feed. Please rest and make yourselves at home. I suspect that you may be weary after the events of the last few days."

Chapter Thirty Three

On the trail to Red River, Hiram had time to think about what might happen if he did find his son. Things came to mind that he had not yet contemplated. He shared his thoughts with Joshua.

"I'm afraid that I hadn't taken time to think this thing through, Joshua. What if I do find my son? He's been with the Comanche longer than he was with Sarah and me. He will be more Comanche than white by now. What if he doesn't even remember me, Joshua?"

Joshua nodded his head as if in agreement. "I suppose that could happen Matthews." He paused and further considered the question. "I remember when I was a kid back in Waco. It used to bother me that the white kids wouldn't accept me. I think something in me wanted to be like them. That old man that taught me English, he knew something was eating on me. He sat me down one day and drug it out of me. Made me talk to him. After I told him what it was eating on me - that I didn't seem to belong anywhere - he told me something. He told me to quit tryin' to be something I wasn't. I can't say that I really understood his advice at the time. Seemed like it was easy for him to say and hard for me to do. But I came round to it. I had a white father, but he was never part of my life. Indian ways and Indian people were what I knew. That's who I am. If you find your boy, he'll have to decide, not you."

"I guess that's what I'm afraid of Joshua."

"Maybe you just have to decide what it is you want, Matthews. We find him; maybe just knowing he's alive should be enough. Maybe he's happy right now just bein' an Indian. Still his decision."

"I guess I just hadn't thought about it till now Joshua. I had told myself before that if Sarah and I could have just known if he were dead or alive it might be easier. If I can find him and see him again, maybe that will be enough. I don't know."

"We gotta find him first, Matthews."

"Yeah." Hiram breathed a sigh. "I know."

The patrol rolled into the Red River Station on time. The station was nothing more than a small outpost with a contingency of only forty troops. Captain Charles White, the fort commander, was anxious for the small patrol of men to return. Communication had been received alerting him of increased hostile activity to the west. He was unprepared to see a civilian and an Indian riding with his patrol. He waited as the Sergeant in charge of the patrol handed him a small leather letter case.

"Sir, I have a letter from Colonel Savage," the Sergeant explained as he handed the Captain the case.

Captain White had still not spoken and he continued to examine Hiram and Joshua as he opened the case and read the communication. When he finished reading, he offered his hand and introduced himself.

"The Colonel has asked me to extend all courtesy to you men," he said. "I am instructed to assist you in any way possible. He does not say in what I am to assist you. I suppose you will be able to explain in due time. I'll have the Sergeant get you settled and we will discuss it all over dinner at my quarters." Captain White was unaccustomed to entertaining Indians, but the Colonel's message had been clear. The welcome extended to both men.

Hiram was beginning to feel that he was finally getting back to his mission. There had been too many distractions and sidetracks. He was anxious to get into Indian Territory and resume his search.

Dinner was promptly at six. The Captain always took dinner at six and he was a stickler for keeping to schedules.

"Mr. Matthews, Joshua, the Colonel indicated that I was to assist you. I'm afraid that he didn't give much explanation as to how. I believe you will have to explain."

"Captain, we are heading into the Territory as soon as possible and then possibly over to Cooper. We were told that most of the non-hostile Comanches are now concentrated up there. We have business among them and we have no idea what to expect."

"You don't strike me as a trader. Any business you may have with the Comanche would have to be conducted through an agent. The Colonel attached a communication to an agent Holmes." He handed Hiram a sealed letter addressed to Agent Benjamin Holmes. "Do you wish to trade goods or to supply beef?"

"Our business is of a different nature. Can you tell us more about the territory and the Comanche there?"

"I don't really know a great deal. There has been limited success in moving the Comanche into the territory. I do know that the conditions are deplorable. There are tribes from a great many of the nations, most of them eastern. There have been outbreaks of smallpox and cholera. Food and supplies are in short supply. The agents up there are doing what they can I suppose. That's why I thought you might be looking to supply cattle."

"A while back that might have been a possibility," Hiram answered. "I'm no longer in the cattle business. I'm afraid that I know nothing about these agents."

"As I understand it, each tribe or nation has agents appointed to help oversee the business of supply and welfare of each. All trading is done through these agents. And I suppose any business you may have will be carried out under their supervision. I have little more to offer than that."

"This agent Holmes, do you know where and how I will find him?"

"The Colonel says in his letter that Holmes operates out of Fort Arbuckle. That's about fifty miles north of here. Cooper is about thirty miles due west."

"Then we would like to get started tomorrow morning if that is possible."

Chapter Thirty Four

Agent Benjamin Holmes had lied, cheated, and stolen his way into an appointment as Indian agent. Although the war had slowed the stream of supplies into the Territory, there was still plenty of money to be made. Blankets, beef, and dry goods of every sort were still being sent into the Territory in spite of the war. There were those supplies intended for the Indian troops who had been recruited into the Confederate army and the supplies intended for the general populace. Complaints concerning shortages of supplies were generally tendered back to the agents themselves so most were never heard. There were good agents that genuinely tried to help the indigenous population, but they were not always the norm. Agents like Holmes could funnel off tremendous caches of contraband, which they would in turn re-sell to the army and the Indian Agency itself through unscrupulous traders and dealers that held contracts with both the Union and Confederacy. It was proving to be a lucrative business. Holmes himself was an unassuming snivel of a man with no conscience, but he was cunning and crafted at finding unscrupulous traders and contractors. The Territory was so far removed from any center of command that stealing was easy and in nearly every instance undetected.

On this particular day Holmes had been notified that several of the elders had requested to speak with him. The territory and everything in it belonged to the native peoples, but Holmes treated it as though it were his private domain. He refused to allow Indians inside his office and would only meet with their elders outside. He made no attempt at learning or understanding anything about the people for whom he was supposed to be responsible. His disdain for the Indian people was unconscionable.

The elders had assembled outside his office where Holmes had intentionally kept them waiting for hours.

Holmes spoke through an interpreter who was on his payroll. "So, what is the complaint today?" he asked.

"Our people have little food. We need blankets. The beef that was promised is never enough to feed all of our people. The medicine that was promised never comes. You promise to sell the goods we produce but we see nothing for our work."

"Look, this is the same old complaint. I've told you people that the war is making it difficult to get supplies in and out. There is nothing that I can do. I've sent your complaints time after time. Nothing changes. It's out of my hands." Holmes lied.

"Our people are hungry and your words and promises do not fill their bellies. You promised white medicine and still our people are dying from sickness."

"I am doing everything I can to see that you get your allotments of clothing, medicine and food. I'm telling you to be patient while I try to sort things out."

There was little the elders could do. They had no weapons, no horses, no way to hunt or fend for themselves. To make matters worse, unscrupulous men were illegally selling whiskey to any Indian with money or anything of value to trade.

"These damn savages never change. We supply them with food, housing, and supplies and all they do is complain," Holmes told his clerk. "The sooner they all die off the better. The whole damn country will be better off."

His clerk was a clueless man that Holmes had hired. He believed anything that he was told and would make a report say whatever Holmes told him it should say. He was good cover for Holmes' operation. Having a clerk who would do what he was told made it look as if everything were on the up and up.

"We have a shipment of goods coming in tomorrow. There will be fifty blankets, a dozen beef cattle, two hundred pounds of corn and beans each, two hundred pounds of flour. You might as well make out the receipt of goods now so I don't have to wait for you to do it tomorrow," he told the hapless clerk.

The supply contractor came in the next day just as planned. The tally of goods given to the clerk was exactly half of what had been appropriated and shipped. Holmes and the contractor had already funneled off their stolen share of the shipment.

"This is almost too easy," Holmes told the contractor. "I'll tell these dumb heathens tomorrow that I got this whole shipment delivered in here just to satisfy their complaints. They'll think I'm some sort of hero."

Chapter Thirty Five

The agency quarters were located some five miles to the west of Fort Arbuckle. The area was dotted with clusters of families organized into small communities. As they rode, the two men could see that the natives were living in generally poor conditions.

"Captain White was right Joshua. Things look pretty bad here."

Joshua remained silent and gave little outward appearance of his reaction to what he was witnessing. Inside he was a turmoil of emotions. He was appalled that once proud civilizations were being reduced to what he was seeing. The hunt was gone. The buffalo were gone. The pride and life was gone from the eyes of so many of the people. The loss that he felt and saw was palpable.

"I believe that would be Holmes office," Hiram said as he pointed to a small building.

The men dismounted and entered the small building. Holmes was seated at a small desk overlooking some paper work. He looked up as the two men entered. His eyes narrowed and he addressed Hiram and Joshua.

"I don't recognize you fellows, so I assume you are strangers here. This office is off limits to Indians. These people are diseased and we're trying to avoid the spread to the agency people. I'll need that Indian to step back outside."

Hiram was totally taken aback at the brashness of the man. He had not been allowed to so much as introduce himself and Joshua before the man had become offensive. He and Joshua stood in the doorway for a moment. Joshua made a motion to turn and leave and Hiram reached out and took Joshua by the arm and shook his head.

"My friend (he stressed the friend) and I are strangers to these parts and we (he stressed the "we") have business with an agent Holmes."

"Well sir, that would be me and I'll still need to insist that the Indian step back outside."

Hiram's anger was beginning to boil. He still held Joshua's arm. Joshua sensed that Hiram was ready to explode.

"It's okay, Matthews. I'll wait outside while you speak with the agent."

Hiram released his grip and calmed himself. He knew that he needed Holmes help, at least for the time being.

"Now, what can I do for you, friend?" Holmes asked. Hiram thought of the confrontation with Mallory back in Waco and what Mallory had said when he had called him friend.

"I have a letter of introduction from a Colonel Savage," he said as he handed the letter to Holmes.

"Can't say I know him well, but I met the man a few years back," Holmes responded as he scanned the document. "He only says that I am to extend my help to you in any way possible. Just exactly what is it that I can do?"

Hiram thought to himself, "You can go to hell where you belong", but restrained himself. "I am looking for my son. I have reason to believe that he may be living here among the Comanche population. He was abducted a number of years ago. We believe by Comanche."

"I see," said Holmes. "And you expect me to help in what way?"

"We could use someone to escort us in our search. Maybe show us the main Comanche encampments."

"I'm not sure that I have anyone who can accompany you. I suggest you get one of their elders to do that. I suppose you may need an interpreter," Holmes said curtly.

"That won't be necessary. My unwelcome friend can handle that. Can you find the elder to help us?"

"I'll send my clerk to fetch one of them. You and your friend can wait outside," Holmes said summarily.

Hiram was pleased to wait outside the office with Joshua. Another minute in the company of Holmes was more than he could stomach.

"I'm sorry for this man's behavior, Joshua. I can't believe he knows Colonel Savage. I dare say Savage knows nothing of the man's character."

"I reckon he's not worth bein' sorry over, Matthews."

"At least he offered to see if an elder was willing to show us around. I guess that's something."

The clerk returned a short time later accompanied by an elder.

"His name's Hayarakwetu Naape. Says people call him Four Toes. He'll help you with whatever you need," said the clerk.

Joshua spoke to the elder in his native tongue and introduced Hiram as "Matthews". He explained the situation to the old man. They spoke back and forth several times.

"Matthews, the old man says there are what he called "White Comanche" living among his people. He says there are three or four that he knows of that fit the description, but there could be others."

"Can he take us to them?" Hiram asked.

Joshua and the old man spoke again. The old man pointed to the horses as he spoke.

"Does he want the horses?"

"Well, he says we will need to ride. Too far to walk."

"Then we'll use one of the pack horses. I'll tell Holmes clerk to watch the gear."

The old man took the men to a small community of Comanche families. He spoke to one of the women present. She departed into a teepee and emerged with a young man. He appeared to be about the right age. His skin was dark from the years of exposure to the sun, but his features were that of a white youth. His hair was a deep black. Hiram knew instinctively that it was not Ethan.

"Tell him that's not the boy, Joshua," Hiram instructed.

They mounted up and the old man took them to another group. The process was repeated with the same result.

"Joshua, tell the old man that the boy we're looking for will have reddish brown hair."

Joshua relayed the information to the old man. He shook his head in a positive reply and motioned for the two to follow him. They rode to the next group of families. As they approached, Hiram could see several people moving about as he scanned the camp for the youth. What he saw caused his heart to freeze for a moment. It was a youth with rusty colored hair sitting at a camp fire with several others. The youth had his back to Hiram and Joshua. Hiram could scarcely believe his eyes. Joshua had also seen the youth.

"You see what I see Matthews?" From the look on Hiram's face he already knew the answer.

They reined their mounts and dismounted. Hiram's heart was racing. One of the other youths looked up and stood. They all turned to see what it was that had caused him to stand. Hiram's heart nearly fell from his chest. The youth's face was badly disfigured on one side. There was no way Hiram could tell for sure if it was Ethan.

"My God, Joshua," he said. "What happened to this boy?"

"Those are burn scars Matthews. May be intentional. May be an accident."

The old man called the youth and motioned for him to come. An Indian woman also approached. Joshua and the old man spoke again.

"The old man says this is the boy's mother."

"Ask her what happened to him."

Joshua questioned the woman and turned to Hiram. "She says he was burned when he was a small child."

"How small Joshua. How long ago?"

"Indians don't count years like white men, but it sounds like the boy would have been four, maybe five. You think this is your boy, Matthews?"

"I just don't know, Joshua," he replied. He turned and went to his saddle bags and withdrew something wrapped in cloth. He came back to the boy and studied his face as he unwrapped the item from the cloth. He withdrew a small hand-carved wooden toy pistol and showed it to the youth. He smiled and said something to his companions. They all laughed.

"What'd he say Joshua?"

"I think he believes you're playing a trick on him. Wants to know why you're showing him a stick."

"Ask him if he's ever seen this before?"

"He says he's seen lots of sticks, Matthews. Never had a crazy old white man offer him one before."

Hiram took another item from the cloth and showed it to the youth. It was a broach on a chain. The youth looked at the item and made a comment.

"He wants to know who the woman is."

"The woman?"

"The woman's face on that bauble. He wants to know who she is."

"Tell him no one, Joshua, no one," he said dejectedly. "It's not him. It's not Ethan."

The men saddled up and rode back to Holmes office in silence. Hiram handed Joshua some money and instructed him to give it to the old man. The old man was grateful for the money and he and Joshua spent several minutes in conversation.

"These people are poor, Joshua. Maybe the money will help. Come on into Holmes office with me and we'll pick up our gear."

Holmes looked up when the two men entered. "I thought I made it clear that his kind are not allowed in here," he said. Hiram was in no mood for any more of Holmes's foolishness. He didn't say a word and walked around the end of Holmes's desk.

"What the hell do you think you're..." He didn't get to finish his sentence. Hiram reached down and grabbed the man by his ears and literally jerked him to his feet. Holmes let out a scream. "You're pulling my ears off you son of a …..." Once again he was unable to finish his sentence. Hiram tightened his grip on his ears even harder and drug him to Joshua. He turned Holmes face to Joshua, still pulling so hard on the man's ears he could feel cartilage breaking.

"Take a good hard look and tell me what you see," he instructed Holmes.

"You're tearing my ears off you son of a ….." Once again Hiram pulled and twisted Holmes ears. Holmes let out another howl.

"Tell me what you see or I promise you, I will tear your ears off."

"I don't know what you mean. Please God, please let go of my ears."

"Tell me what you see."

"Okay, okay. I see an Indian." Holmes yowled.

Hiram tightened his grip once again and could feel blood on his fingertips. Holmes let out another scream.

"Try again and get it right. I believe I feel one of your ears tearing off."

"Your friend. I see your friend."

"That's right," Hiram replied. "You see my friend, not "that Indian, not "his kind". You see my friend. He served the State of Texas honorably as a scout. He saved my life and the life of a number of army troops down in Texas. Now you remember his face. That's what a friend's face looks like." He released his grip on Holmes ears.

"You nearly pulled my ears off you old son of a b…..."

He never saw what hit him. The lights went out as Hiram's fist slammed into his jaw. "I'll have words with the Colonel about you."

Joshua repacked the gear and the two men rode away from Holmes office.

"I'm sorry it wasn't Ethan, Hiram." Joshua said as they rode away.

The two rode south in silence. Joshua was content to allow Hiram time to deal with the events of the day. That evening as they sat by a camp fire Joshua felt it was time to ask.

"What was all that with the wooden pistol and the bauble?"

"I carved that pistol for Ethan when he was only a few years old. It was his favorite toy. When he disappeared we found it down by the creek. The broach belonged to Sarah, and Ethan was always fascinated with it. He would play with it when he was in his Mother's lap. I'm certain that Ethan would remember either of the two items. That young boy had no idea what they were."

Joshua considered what Hiram had told him. "What are we going to do now? There's still the area around the Pease." Joshua offered.

"I can't ask you to go there with me. You heard what Savage said. It's unstable and could be dangerous not knowing what we could be getting into."

"Well, I ain't scared of a few Indians. And I spoke to the old man about any Comanche settlements on the Pease. He thinks there are maybe only two or three villages over toward the head waters. He thinks they are probably friendlies. We've come all this way. No sense in turning back now and you can't go it alone without an interpreter. Who knows, we might just get a look at one of those big buffalo herds that are up here somewhere. Besides, like I told ya before, you ….."

"Yeah, I know, I ain't got good survival skills. So, we head southwest toward the Pease."

Chapter Thirty Six

The upper Pease lay close to the Escarpment area of Texas. The two lone riders had seen the landscape gradually change into slightly rolling prairie terrain. It yielded little change as far as the eye could see. There was the occasional lone tree except in the river bottoms and miles of sagebrush and grass. The weather had grown steadily hotter as the men traveled. Even though it was only early May, the Texas sun was unrelenting. The men had headed steadily southwest back toward the Red River. They knew they could follow the Red to where the Pease emptied into the big river. They would never be more than about one hundred miles from Fort Cooper.

"I wouldn't want to be up here by mid-summer, Hiram. There's nowhere to get out of this heat."

"I expect it will be pretty harsh by the end of the month. If that elder was right I don't think we'll be here all that long. If there are only a few villages and they are concentrated around the upper Pease like he said; we find Ethan or not, we should be headed back south in only a week or so. To tell you the truth, I'm out of ideas where to look if something doesn't pan out up here. I just hope I don't get us both scalped. And even if we get lucky enough to find one village, how will we know if we're riding into a friendly camp or not?"

"I think ya' have to leave that to me, Hiram. We sure as heck can't just go riding into any village like we own the place. I think this is where I earn my money. We go slow, we locate the villages, and I go in alone. I think I will be better received than a white man. We just gotta be patient."

"I can't say I like the idea of you being out there on your own. What if you go riding into an unfriendly bunch?"

"I can probably pass for Comanche, Hiram. I speak the language. Hell, don't I look like an Indian?"

"Maybe so, Joshua. But I still don't like the idea."

"Either way, we gotta find them first. No guarantees that they haven't already moved into the territory or further north. The Comanche that the old man spoke of could be anywhere by now. This may be the last place on earth they could still be following the buffalo. If that's the case, we may never find them."

By the third day out the pair had crossed the Red and were following the south edge of a long, deep canyon that had been carved by the Pease over thousands of years. They could see the layers of colored red, brown, and yellow-green earth in the canyon walls that revealed centuries of climate change. The two men had searched the horizon for movement or smoke from a fire, but there had been no indication of life for several days. On the morning of the fourth day Joshua spotted what appeared to be a small wisp of smoke.

"There," he pointed. A small column of blue gray extended from the horizon. "That's smoke, Hiram."

"If that's one of their camps, we won't be able to get within a country mile before we're seen."

"I think we have to risk getting closer to tell. It's impossible to say what we're looking at. Could be a hunting party. Could be a camp."

Two miles away the raiding party was preparing to move north back into the territory. Their raids on settlers on the Brazos and Wichita to the south had been successful. They had stolen a dozen horses and burned out several isolated families.

Hiram and Joshua had slowly worked their way toward the area where they had seen the smoke column. They were still a mile out when they found a small draw deep enough to conceal a rider and mount. The raiding party was still totally unaware of the approaching riders.

Joshua pointed to the draw and reined his mount toward the cover of the low area. "I think this will be a good spot for you to stay with the pack horses. It won't provide any cover in a fight, but it will have to do. I'll ride on in from here and have a look."

"If anything doesn't look or feel right you hightail it back here."

Joshua nodded an affirmative and headed up from the shallow draw. He was no more than a half mile from the group of raiders when he was spotted. One of the warriors let out a whoop and pointed. It was unfortunate for Joshua that the party was only interested in taking horses and loot. Had that not been the case they probably would have waited to see who was approaching. As it was, what they saw was a lone rider and another horse for the taking. A dozen of the warriors quickly mounted and charged in Joshua's direction. Joshua realized immediately that they were not coming to extend a hand of welcome. He wheeled and kicked his mount. Hiram was watching from the crest of the little draw and saw Joshua turn. He quickly mounted and spurred his horse but the pack animals slowed him down. Joshua was quickly narrowing the distance between him and Hiram. They were soon side by side with their mounts running flat out. They heard the rifle repeats and heard the bullets as they whizzed by their heads. The canyon was on their right and the open plain was on their left. There was nothing to do but to try to outrun their pursuers in the hope that they would break off their attack.

"We hang on to these pack horses, we can't outrun this bunch," Hiram shouted at Joshua.

"Then cut 'em loose. They may break off the chase."

Hiram dropped the lead string of the pack horses and they continued to run but began to drop back. The pursuers continued the chase and soon overtook the pack animals. Two of the pursuers dropped out to secure the horses. The remaining warriors continued to bear down on Hiram and Joshua.

"We're trapped here Joshua. There's no cover anywhere," Hiram shouted.

"We've got to find something. One of this bunch is gonna get lucky with those rifles and hit one of us or our mount."

"Look for any pocket at the edge of the canyon," Hiram shouted. He reached back and untied his saddle bags and slung them over his shoulder.

The raiders were closing and were still firing wildly. Hiram and Joshua sped along the edge of the cliff when they spotted a small area where water had eroded the edge of the canyon forming a small ragged depression. He pointed and motioned to Joshua.

Just as they sprang from their mounts a bullet hit Joshua's mount and it fell. Joshua was almost free of the saddle, but the fall partially threw him. He was half running and half falling toward the edge of the cliff trying to gain his balance. Hiram had jumped from his mount and he threw himself in front of Joshua in a flying tackle and both men went down. They scrambled on all fours into the little niche. They were almost hanging from the edge of the cliff but the niche provided cover from the rifle fire of the pursuers.

"I think I was about to find out if I could fly. Good thing you tackled me."

Joshua's mount was badly wounded and still struggling to get to its feet. His prized bow and canteen hung from the saddle. The raiders had closed to well within rifle range. Hiram squeezed off a shot and one rider fell. The warriors realized that they were easy targets and broke off the attack. Two more broke away from the group and had soon claimed Hiram's mount. Two of the warriors decided to show their bravery and sped directly at Hiram and Joshua. Both men fired and missed. Before they could get off another shot the two were on them. One warrior sprang from his mount and threw himself directly at Joshua in a flying tackle. Both men tumbled perilously close to the cliff edge. Hiram drew his pistol and fired. The second warrior went down and tumbled at Hiram's feet. Joshua was struggling with the other warrior and both men had their knives drawn. The man broke free of Joshua's grasp and knocked Joshua to his back and he slid ever closer to the cliff edge. Hiram was looking for an opportunity to get a clear shot. The warrior sprang at Joshua, knife drawn. Joshua was still on his back but was able to catch the assailant mid-section with both feet. He catapulted the man over his body and the warrior flew screaming over the edge of the cliff.

Joshua scrambled to his feet and both men turned their attention to the other warriors.

"You hurt, Joshua?"

"No. Damned lucky that one jumped at me like he did though."

"We've got to put that animal down and try to get that canteen, Joshua."

"Yeah, and I want my bow."

Hiram took aim and with one shot the animal was down. The raiders remained at the edge of rifle range. The two riders returned to the group with Hiram's mount in tow and began to whoop and shout. They fired their rifles into the air as they galloped away with their prize. Hiram and Joshua watched from their position as the group rode away.

"Can't say I expected that to happen Joshua. I guess they weren't looking for scalps."

"Probably a raiding party looking for horses. These two were trying to show the others how brave they were. Bad choice. But the rest of them could come back with all their friends. They may wait till dark."

"I didn't think Indians would fight in the dark."

"That's one of those stupid white man fables. Comanche don't much care what time of day it is if they're lookin' for scalps."

"I don't know, but we've been here before. We're walking again!" He looked down at his side and winced. Joshua had not noticed that Hiram had been hit. When he saw Hiram wince with pain he looked down and saw the blood beginning to stain his shirt.

"You hit?"

"I am. Hadn't really felt it till now."

"Let me have a look." Joshua pulled the shirt back and saw where a bullet had entered Hiram's side. "You want the good news first?"

"What the heck can be good about a bullet wound?"

"Well, it looks like it just barely caught your side and the bullet went through. You in much pain?"

"It hurts like the devil, but I'll live. What's the bad news?"

"You're still bleeding. We ain't going anywhere till we get that stopped. We have my canteen and we've got our rifles. I'm guessing Cooper is close to a hundred miles south, south east. I think that's where we've got to go. We head south and pick up the Brazos we should find Cooper easy enough. First we gotta get you fit to travel. But we ain't goin' anywhere till we see if that bunch is coming back." He paused as if in thought. "You partial to horse meat, Hiram?"

"Horse meat?"

"Yeah. Horse meat. You shot my horse. She is definitely dead and I'm hungry. We might as well get something out of it! I think I can round up enough sticks to make a fire - that is if you have any of those sulfur matches left in those saddle bags. First we gotta make some sort of bandage for that wound and get that bleeding stopped."

"Well, I don't fancy squatting around here waiting to heal, but I suppose we don't have a choice. I guess we can get moving tomorrow. I just hope that bunch don't come back."

"All right. You sit and we'll get you patched up We'll wait a spell to see if we're gonna have company again. Then I'll get a fire going." Joshua quickly harvested a small piece of horse flesh from the hind of the horse and prepared to make a fire.

The raiding party had regrouped. They had realized that the two men had nowhere to go. The cliff was at their back and the open prairie would provide no cover. They decided that the two would be easy to kill, but they would need the cover of night.

Hiram and Joshua were still in the cover of the small depression at the cliff edge when they saw the group coming back. There appeared to be about a dozen warriors. The raiders were careful to stay well out of rifle range. It quickly became apparent to the two men that it had now become a waiting game.

"What do you reckon they have planned for us, Joshua?"

"Probably waitin' till dark. They know they can't hit us till then. Looks like we get to eat this horse meat raw."

"I don't know that we can survive an all out attack. If they hit us in the dark from two sides, they'll be all over us. I've only got about a dozen rounds for the pistol and we've got what's in the rifles."

"They've got us in a bad spot, Hiram. We can wait' em out, but you're right. They come at us in the dark from two ways, we're dead."

"Well I ain't fond of the idea of going hand to hand with this bunch."

"The way I see it, we've got one way out. We have to climb down, if you're up to it. I'm gonna get the rope off my horse. It might come in handy. Keep an eye on 'em while I crawl out there and get it. We have to get down before dark."

"I'm no climber, Joshua. Hell, we might as well wait 'em out as to fall and kill ourselves."

"No way, Hiram. We stay here, we're dead for sure. There's too many of em."

Hiram considered the options for a moment. He crawled to the canyon edge and looked down. The first twenty feet was a jagged drop off. He shook his head. "This is nuts, but get the rope. There is a ledge about twenty feet down. If we can make that, maybe we can pick our way down."

"I'll see if I can get down to that ledge. You may want to take those boots off and tie 'em around your neck, Hiram. We'll have to sling our rifles with a bit of rope. Just try to follow my lead. If I fall, don't go that way."

"Very funny, Joshua."

Joshua eased over the edge of the canyon feeling with his feet for any footing. He found that the jagged rock face actually provided fairly easy access. He continued to work his way down. Hiram watched from above and eased himself over the edge trying to follow Joshua's lead. They soon found themselves standing on the small ledge.

"That wasn't as bad as it looked." Hiram said bravely trying to bolster his confidence.

"Don't get too excited yet, Hiram. We've got another hundred feet or more to go." He studied the path of the ledge and pointed to their left. "Looks like we can work our way over to the big rock at the end of the ledge. I don't know where we go from there. We just have to keep moving. We're easy targets if that bunch decides not to wait, and we're running out of daylight."

They placed their backs to the canyon wall and edged toward the rock. Footing was good and they reached the rock safely. They were at what appeared to be a dead end. They could see clearly that going back would end in another dead end. Joshua lay down on the rock and scooted to the edge to get a look.

"Looks like there's another small ledge about fifteen feet down, but this rock's hanging out over it. No way to climb down to it."

They considered their next move. Joshua began to formulate an idea. He found a split in the rock face and jammed his rifle, muzzle first, into the opening.

"What are you doing?" Hiram asked.

"One of us has to go down on the rope and try to swing in to that little ledge. You can't lower me. Your side's bleeding again and I don't know if I can hold you. But if I can jam this rifle into this crack good enough, I think I can loop the rope around the barrel and use that to help hold you."

"What happens if I can't swing in to the ledge?"

"Well, I hope I can hoist you back up. You got any better suggestions?"

"How do you get down?"

"If you can get onto that ledge, you've got to find a way to tie off your end of the rope. I think we can double it around the rifle, and I can climb down on the opposite end of the rope. Once I'm down, we pull the free end of the rope down. We lose the rifle, but we keep the rope."

"Then let's figure out how to jam that rifle into that crack where it will stay. If I have to think about this too much, I may decide to jump and get it over with."

They worked the rifle muzzle deeper into the crack and it appeared it would hold. Hiram formed a loop in the rope end and looped it around himself.

Joshua readied himself and Hiram eased over the edge. Joshua felt the rope tighten and then felt Hiram's full weight on the rope. He slowly began to feed rope as he inched Hiram down.

"Hold it right there." Hiram relayed when he felt he was in position to attempt to swing onto the ledge.

Joshua held fast as Hiram began to attempt to swing himself toward the ledge. After several moments of kicking his legs back and forth he began to swing toward the ledge. It was no more than eight feet away. He reached out as he swung toward the ledge. His hand found the canyon wall but he failed to get a grasp. He continued to swing back and forth. After several attempts his hand found a small crack and he held fast. The ledge was only a foot or two below his feet.

"Ease me down, Joshua," he yelled up to his friend.

Joshua eased him down and his feet found solid ground. "I'm down," he yelled again.

Joshua relaxed his grip on the rope and waited. Hiram looked for any place he could find to tie the rope end. There appeared to be no place onto which he could tie the rope. He examined the crack that he caught when he swung to the ledge. It wasn't deep enough to jam his rifle into. He quickly tied a large knot in the end of the rope and jammed it into the crack at a narrow spot above a wider opening. "Toss down the end of the rope," he yelled to Joshua. He grabbed the loose end and pulled himself up until his full weight was on the rope. The knot held fast in the crack of the rock. He decided that it was as good as it was going to get. "It's chancey, but I think I've got this end secure. Whenever you're ready," he yelled again. "Good Lord, we can use some help here," he murmured and placed his hands against the knot to help keep it in place.

Joshua prepared himself to begin the descent. He pulled at the rope to test the hold. It seemed to be tight. He eased over the edge and began to slide down the rope. He was dangling in midair over a long drop even with the shelf.

Hiram instructed Joshua to try to swing toward the ledge. The knotted rope still held fast. He held fast to the crack with one hand as he extended his rifle out. Joshua began to kick his legs and swung slowly toward the ledge. He grabbed at the rifle muzzle and missed. On the next try he grabbed the end of the rifle. Hiram pulled him toward the ledge and he found footing. When his weight lifted from the rope the knot turned loose from the crack.

"You said it was chancey, Hiram, not crazy!"

"Well, it worked and you're down aren't you?"

They pulled the rope down and rested a moment. They examined their new position and after a few minutes Hiram pointed to their right. "If we can climb down to that rock flow over there, we can almost slide the rest of the way down on that loose rock."

They began picking their way down and to the right and were soon at the top of a long, sloping slide. The surface was covered with small, loose rocks and sandy particles underneath. They stood for a moment considering their final leg of descent. They looked at one another and nodded their heads. In unison they jumped into the loose gravel and rock. They half slid and half ran down the loose, sloping surface and soon tumbled to a halt at the base of the flow. They were safely at the valley floor.

When the warriors crept to the little niche under the cover of darkness, they found their prey had vanished.

Chapter Thirty Seven

Amos Stanford and his company of hunters had been following the big herd of bison on their movement to the south for days. The hunting had been good from the Canadian down and their wagons were already laden with hides, but there were more for the taking. The demand for leather and hides was strong in Europe and America. Hides were going for three dollars each and a good hide with a full winter coat of hair could fetch fifty dollars in some markets. Amos Stanford was well aware of that fact.

He had been a successful businessman in Chicago but had seen the huge potential for wealth in the hide market. With a substantial bankroll in hand he had put together a successful hiding enterprise in Texas. He could have run the business through a hired manager, but had chosen to come to Texas and personally accompany his hunters and entourage. He was a wealthy adventurer and entrepreneur and he liked to travel in style. He had commissioned the construction of a specially designed coach that he had brought to Texas for his comfort on the hunts. His company was almost a small traveling city with cooks, blacksmiths, marksmen, re-loaders, skinners, loaders, armed riders and wagon teamsters. It took a lot of hides to pay the expenses for such a group, but several wet years in Texas had seen a recovery in the quantity and quality of the animals and this hunt was going to be a huge financial success.

On this particular morning Stanford was discussing the hunt with his pusher.

"How far ahead do you think the herd pushed when they spooked, Mr. Horn?"

"They have crossed the Pease, but I think no more than a day or two Mr. Stanford," Horn replied nervously. He knew that

Stanford was unhappy that one of his marksmen had spooked the herd when he had wounded an animal with a poor shot. Stanford was not a vindictive man, but he held high expectations of others and had little tolerance for failure.

"Tell Mr. Givings that I will dock him a week's wages for the lost time. Time is money, Mr. Horn."

"Yes, sir. I'll tell him."

"I'll be docking you a week as well, Mr. Horn."

Horn started to object and thought better of it. "Yes, sir," he replied.

Stanford sensed that Horn was unhappy with being held complicit for an errant shot. "Does that seem harsh to you, Mr. Horn?"

"Mr. Stanford, I know you're a fair man. But, yes sir, it does seem harsh to dock us a week's pay. I hire good people and I have to trust them to do their job. I don't know a single hunter that don't make an occasional bad shot. It happens. I think the men all trust you to be fair. That's all."

"I agree, Mr. Horn. I don't want trust issues either and I appreciate you standing up for your men. I pay good wages and expect good performance. But I believe that was Mr. Giving's second miss on this hunt. He was fortunate the first time. The herd didn't spook. I kept quiet on that one. He's your man. You control his performance. You will both lose the week's wages. If Mr. Givings wishes, he may plead his case with me. Although, I can't say that I recommend it."

"Yes, sir," Horn replied sheepishly.

"Now, that business being concluded, where do we stand on the hunt?"

"We'll cross the Pease tomorrow and I think we can be in position by the day after to harvest more hides. We have fifteen wagons at full load of two hundred fifty hides each. We have five wagons yet to fill. If all goes well it should take only about three

The Redemption of Hiram Matthews

days tops and we're loaded out. We should have around five thousand hides."

"Very well, Mr. Horn. Tell the men that I will give them one dollar per hide bonus to be split among the crew for everything over the five thousand. I will pay an additional five dollars per hide with a good winter coat. Will the wagons support more than the two hundred each?"

"We'll figure out how to make the load work Mr. Stanford. But this late in the year I'm afraid there will be few with full coats."

"Let's get the company moving Mr. Horn."

Chapter Thirty Eight

Hiram and Joshua had been walking south for two days. They had worked their way out of the canyon and onto the surrounding prairie. The flat prairie was waist high in needle grass and it had made going slow and difficult. A mild late season norther had moved in dropping the temperature several degrees and a slow, drizzling rain had been falling for hours. Although not severe, Hiram's wound had not been given a chance to heal, and the bleeding had continued off and on. He could feel his strength giving way, and he was beginning to feel feverish. He knew he was slowing their progress and had begun to fear that he would soon be unable to walk any farther.

"Joshua, I don't know how much farther I can go. I'm feeling worse with every step, and I feel like I'm freezing."

"We need to find a place to get out of this weather and let you rest up for a while, and we need to do it before dark, Hiram. It's gonna get colder tonight. We could use some good luck for a change."

"I'm good for a few more miles maybe, Joshua. I won't make any promises."

They continued their walk through the deep grass for another hour. The prairie floor had risen almost imperceptibly for the entire hour. Joshua had noted that the horizon seemed to be drawing closer and they were actually walking uphill. At the end of the hour the men came to the crest of the small rise and the prairie sloped away. The sight before their eyes was almost unbelievable. What they saw was a virtual sea of bones; the aftermath of a by-gone slaughter of hundreds of buffalo. Both men stood silently as they surveyed the field of bones.

"My God, Joshua. There must be hundreds of skeletons."

"Work of white buffalo hunters. Indians wouldn't have killed like this. These animals were left to rot after they were killed. Looks like it must have happened a while ago."

"How can people do this kind of thing, Joshua?"

Joshua was sick to his stomach, but he was still thinking survival. "I don't know. But this may be exactly what we need. I can make a shelter from these bones and this grass. It'll take a while and I'll need as much help as you can give me."

"What do you need me to do?"

"If you're up to it, use your knife and start cutting clumps of grass. I'll start making a framework."

Joshua set to work immediately gathering the large rib bones from the skeletons. When he had enough to build a framework, he cut his rope into sections and began to unravel it to use in binding the bones together. In an amazingly short time he had built a respectable framework that would hold the grass covering. Hiram had harvested a fair amount of grass, but all the movement had opened his wound again.

"I've got it from here Hiram. You need to set down and let me finish this thing."

Another hour passed as Joshua continued to cover the framework with grass. He had padded the floor with the soft prairie grass and the two men now had a warm, semi-dry place to rest. They crawled in and lay on their backs.

"I wish we had some of those hides. Another piece of that horse meat wouldn't be all that bad either."

Hiram was too spent to answer. He lay on his back looking at the inside of the makeshift shelter. He was thankful to be out of the cold rain and was tired to the bone. The fever and chills had worsened. They both soon drifted into an uneasy sleep.

Joshua dreamed that he was on the prairie. He was sitting on his pony watching a huge herd of buffalo, but he was old and the buffalo were all white. An old man sat on another pony and spoke in his native tongue.

"What do you see?" the old man asked.

"I see the Buffalo grandfather. Why are they white?" he asked the old man.

"You see only the ghosts of the buffalo."

"Are they the ghosts of the dead buffalo whose bones we saw?"

"They are the ghosts of all buffalo."

"Why do I see only their ghosts?"

"You see only the ghosts because the buffalo are no more."

"But if they are no more, what will become of the people?"

"Soon the people will become as the buffalo and they too will be no more."

Chapter Thirty Nine

Joshua could still hear the buffalo from his dream. They grunted and called to one another as they fed on the prairie grasses. Their sound was growing louder as he began to rouse from sleep. He opened his eyes and stared at the ceiling of the little shelter. He thought of the dream. "That was some dream," he thought. "I can still hear the buffalo." His head was still clearing from sleep, but the sound of the buffalo remained. He lay still and listened. "I know I'm awake. Why in the devil do I think I still hear buffalo?"

Hiram was still sleeping and Joshua nudged him. He slowly began to wake.

"How ya feelin'?" he asked.

"I'm some better. I slept some, and the chills seem to be gone." His head was beginning to clear and he was fully awake. "What's all that noise? It almost sounds like cattle."

"I thought I was hearing things. I dreamed about buffalo and can't get the sound out of my head."

Joshua pushed back the grass covering the shelter entry and scooted out. What he saw when he stood up he could scarcely believe. There were buffalo everywhere. He and Hiram were within a hundred feet of an enormous herd that spread out over the plain for what appeared to be a mile or more.

"Hiram, get out here. You gotta see this."

Hiram scooted out and stood. He was still weak from the fever and thought for a moment that he was having some sort of illusion.

"Good Lord, Joshua. I've seen a few buffalo, but never anything like this. There must be a hundred thousand or more of them. I've heard people talk about them, but this is beyond what I could have imagined. I thought the big herds were probably all gone by now."

"I expect that will happen soon enough. An old man in my dream last night told me so."

They stood watching the animals for several minutes. It finally dawned on Hiram that they were dangerously close to the big herd.

"This is quite a sight, Joshua, but we might want to see if we can put a little distance between us and them. If that herd were to spook and turn our direction, I think we would be in trouble. One of those big bulls could decide to take a run at us."

"Agreed. You okay to start moving?"

"I expect I'll be good for a bit but I'm kinda weak."

They began to work their way along the top of the rise. They were no more than fifteen feet above the sloping floor of the prairie, but they could see a good distance. The herd of buffalo seemed to stretch for a mile or more. A band of brown against the light green of the prairie grass. They stood surveying the herd and made the sighting almost at the same time. The movement was miles away on the far side of the big herd but in the flat terrain it was easy to spot from their slightly elevated position.

Joshua squinted against the morning sun. "That's movement, Hiram. I'm not sure, but that may be wagons."

"You think it could be military?"

"No way to know from this distance. Can't tell which direction they're headed. If they're moving away we can't possibly catch up to 'em. They could hear a rifle shot, but that might spook this big herd. We have to try to get their attention somehow; but how?"

"If we could get a fire going we could use the smoke, but we got nothing to start a fire. We used your last match," Joshua replied.

Hiram's mind was racing. There's got to be a way. He stood thinking for a moment. "Give me that canteen. It's metal underneath that cloth cover." He quickly used his knife to strip away the canteen covering. The metal underneath was tarnished tin. "Damn, it's not bright enough." he said. He tore a small portion of fabric from his shirt and scooped up a handful of the prairie sand. He began to scour the surface of the canteen and after a few minutes the tarnish had yielded and the canteen surface was shining. Hiram directed the canteen face toward the sun and moved it back and forth.

"If anybody down there is watching maybe they'll see the glint from the canteen."

Almost two miles away John Horn was watching. Something shiny caught his eye. He stopped and stared in the direction of the light. It flashed again and again. Horn spurred his mount to Stanford's coach.

"Mr. Stanford, I'm picking up something shining toward the south east."

"Something shining?" Stanford replied.

"Yes, sir. Sun's reflecting off something. Whatever it is doesn't seem to be moving. It's coming from the same place every time."

"Indians, Mr. Horn?"

"I don't much think so Mr. Stanford. I don't think Indians would give themselves away like that. It was almost like whatever, or whoever it is – well it's like it's on purpose."

"Do you mean like a signal of some sort, Mr. Horn?"

"Could be, sir. Watch right out there."

Stanford looked in the direction indicated and he picked up a faint flash. It flickered and disappeared almost in a timed rhythm.

"Could be military," he said. "Send three of the guards to see what it is."

Joshua and Hiram continued to signal with the canteen. They watched intently in the direction of the wagons for any indication that someone had spotted them. After several minutes had passed they spotted the riders. They were still a mile away, but they were headed straight toward Hiram and Joshua. The riders closed the distance quickly and in only a few minutes they sat staring at the two men.

"You fellas forget where you left your horses or ya just out for a walk?"

"Out for a walk," Hiram replied. "We ran into a little bunch of scrappers. They wanted our horses and we wanted our scalps. They got the horses."

"Well, climb on up and we'll take you to meet Mr. Stanford. He's our boss."

Chapter Forty

Stanford had sat on his coach watching intently as the riders approached.

"Mr. Stanford, we checked like you said and we found these two fellas out there. It was them you saw."

Joshua and Hiram slipped from the riders mounts.

"I'm Hiram Matthews and this is my friend Joshua. We tangled with a small raiding party a couple of days ago. Lost everything except our hair."

"I'm Amos Stanford and this little enterprise you see is mine. It appears that you have been bleeding Mr. Matthews. Are you hurt?"

"Yes, I am. Took a round through my side. It's still giving me some problems."

"We have a man that can take a look at that for you. He's not a doctor, but he has some knowledge. I believe you should climb aboard and I'll put you in my quarters for now. Joshua, was it? You'll have to stay with the men. I'm afraid there isn't room in the coach. You are a Native American are you not? I would guess Kiowa."

"That's right, Mr. Stanford. But I am Huaco. Is that important?"

"Not for me, but it might be for the men. I'll make sure you are well received." He turned to John Horn, who had come to hear what was happening. "Mr. Horn, I trust that you can make Joshua comfortable."

"Yes, sir. I'll see to it." Horn knew that Stanford would frown on any failure.

"Very well. And please have Mr. Wright report to my coach to take a look at Mr. Matthews." He turned his attention to Hiram once again. "When Mr. Wright is through checking you out, we will speak further, Mr. Matthews. Now, let's get you aboard and let Mr. Wright do his work."

Wright finished his examination of Hiram and reported to Stanford.

"That fella' probably has an infection in that wound. He feels feverish. I cleaned his wound and disinfected it with whiskey. It may have to be cauterized."

"Did you inform Mr. Matthews?"

"No sir. He's resting right now. I think he's pretty weak."

"Then we will let him rest. Please keep an eye on him for now." He turned to Mr. Horn. "Mr. Matthew's friend is invited to take this evening's meal with me. I think I would enjoy hearing his account of what befell them."

Stanford's company made camp within a half mile of the big buffalo herd. Harvesting of the big animals would commence the following morning. Joshua watched as preparations were being made. He didn't like what he saw. He knew that the morning would bring the slaughter of hundreds of buffalo. Horn had informed him that he was to take supper with Stanford. By the evening Hiram had begun to feel better, but Mr. Wright had recommended that he stay in bed to rest. Joshua was on his own with Stanford. The table was set outside Stanford's coach, complete with a linen tablecloth. Joshua had no desire to be in the man's company, but felt it would be rude to snub the man who had shown hospitality to him and Hiram.

"I trust that Mr. Horn has you set up in one of the tents for the night."

"He has. We're grateful for your help."

"I hope the meal will be to your liking, Joshua."

"The last one we had was raw horse meat, so I expect anything will top that."

After the meal, Stanford was anxious to learn more about his guests.

"I'm curious. Do you have a last name, Joshua?"

"Never felt I needed one." Joshua replied.

"Then Joshua it is. Tell me how you and Mr. Matthews came to be afoot in the middle of the prairie."

"We ran into a small raiding party or maybe a hunting party. I didn't stop to ask them. We had to make a run for it. Hiram had to let our pack animals go, and we lost our mounts when we took cover."

"And where were you bound when you were attacked?"

"We were headed toward the headwaters of the Pease. We were let to believe there were settlements of Comanche there. Possibly friendly."

"I believe you said that you are of the Huaco culture. Why would you be seeking Comanche? Are you somehow related?"

Joshua gave Stanford the short version of why he and Hiram were looking for the Comanche.

"I think that you and Mr. Matthews were in for some disappointment, Joshua. Our company took the hides you saw from up on the Canadian. We followed the big herd south and passed through the area where you were headed. There are non-hostiles, but not on the Pease. I believe they all followed the big herd north to the Canadian. Had you found Comanche I doubt they would have been receptive to guests! Your bad luck running into that small party may have turned out to be not so bad luck after all."

"How can you be so sure that all the Comanche moved north?"

"I suppose there could still be isolated bands. This is a vast country so no one could be certain, but I have serious doubt that you and Mr. Matthews would have found what you seek."

"I guess Hiram knew this was a hard trail we're on."

"I've never had children. I suppose I have no idea how far a man would go to find his son."

"My observation has been that it's pretty far."

The conversation died for a moment. Stanford and Joshua both felt the tension in the air.

At length Stanford broke the silence. "I assume you know what will take place tomorrow morning."

"I guess I'd be pretty dull if I didn't."

"And you do not approve?"

"Mr. Stanford, I reckon that what you do is really not any of my business, but I'm not obliged to agree with it."

"I think I can understand your feelings on the matter, given your heritage. What we are doing is business my friend. Nothing more, nothing less. I'm a capitalist. Money makes the world go round and those buffalo out there, they're money all wrapped up in a big brown hide."

"I don't believe I know what a capitalist is, Mr. Stanford. But I guess that must be someone who values money above most everything else."

"It's not the money, Joshua. It's what the money can do. Nothing of any import happens without money. Sooner or later the war will be over and there will be a nation to be rebuilt. It will take money and men who know how to use it to make that happen. There will be fantastic opportunities to supply goods and services to the nation as it grows. The expansion will be to the west. If a man is in position to supply the needs the opportunity is almost limitless. Hides are just one commodity that happen to be in high demand now. That could change, so I'm making the most of the market while it exists."

"What about the people who have always depended on the buffalo. People like you are destroying our way of life. My people were buffalo hunters. The buffalo are disappearing and so are the native people."

"One of the misfortunes of progress, Joshua. You said your people were buffalo hunters." He stressed the "were". I assume that means they no longer follow the herds. People adapt and change or they disappear."

"Maybe what you're saying is true. I don't have to like it."

"What about your future Joshua? I could put a good man like you to work."

"I've got a job. I work for Hiram."

"Speaking of Mr. Matthews; I think we should check on your friend."

Chapter Forty One

Hiram's condition was greatly improved by the following morning. The whiskey had cleansed the wound sufficiently to stem the growth of the infection. Wright was satisfied that cauterizing the wound would no longer be necessary and had stitched the wound quite well for an untrained man.

"You're a strong individual, Mr. Matthews. You seem to have the constitution of an ox. We'll need to keep that bandage clean and change it once a day, but I see no reason to doubt that you will be fine."

"I appreciate what you have done for us. I don't know what might have happened had you not come along."

Stanford chimed in. "I'm pleased that you were able to get our attention. That was a stroke of genius to use the canteen as a signaling device. You're a man that can think on his feet, Mr. Matthews. My business could use a man of your caliber. I've already tried to hire your friend but he turned me down flat. He says he is in your employ. If you came to work for me perhaps I could get him to reconsider."

"Mr. Stanford, I appreciate the offer. I know Joshua has shared my story with you. He tells me that heading back to the Pease would likely be a bust."

"I believe that to be true, Mr. Matthews. Why don't you abandon this quest? Texas is as big as an ocean. Finding your son in that vast area is impossible. I can offer you and Joshua a future. Why not consider it?"

"I don't know for sure what I want to do now. The cattle business is what I know. I do know for certain that I want to go home once more. After that, I can't say."

"Were you a wrangler?"

"I had a successful cattle ranch."

"All the better, Mr. Matthews. The buffalo are being over hunted. We are forced to travel greater distances on every hunt. This market will dry up before long. Cattle are where the future lies. When this war ends the expansion will be west. Mark my word, sooner than later the railroads will extend into Texas. Instead of big drives, cattle will go to the markets by rail. We'll be able to access markets for top dollar. People will need goods and supplies. If a man is positioned correctly there are fortunes to be made. You know cattle, and I have capital. Perhaps you would be open to some sort of partnership in a cattle operation?"

"Mr. Stanford, you move pretty fast. You don't know me or anything about me and you're talking partnerships?"

"I know enough Mr. Matthews. I know what you've given up to look for your son. That speaks volumes about your pluck, character, and determination. And like you just said, you know cattle." Stanford paused and stroked his chin. "Joshua didn't say. Where would home be?"

"South of here, down close to Waco."

"I know Waco. Once we are loaded out with hides we will head toward Dallas. We float the hides down the Trinity. You can acquire horses and supplies in Dallas. Unfortunately, I haven't saddles and mounts to spare so you are stuck with us until then. That gives us time to get to know one another better and to talk more about the cattle business."

The next morning found the marksmen positioned to begin taking the buffalo. Joshua and Hiram sat at a distance watching the operation begin. The shooters were armed with large bore Sharp's rifles that could be accurate up to five hundred yards and greater. The shooters were stationed at distances that prevented the report of the rifles from spooking the herd, except when a shot failed to take an animal down.

The three shooters commenced the harvest an hour after day break. The big animals fell one after another as the remainder of the herd continued to feed on the prairie grasses seemingly unaware of what was taking place. The prairie was soon littered with the bodies of the fallen animals. As the herd drifted away from the fallen animals, the skinners moved in with the teams of mules. Joshua and Hiram watched as the steel spikes were driven through the snouts of the dead animals. The skinners then made the required cuts. The hides were tied off to the harnesses of the mules, and the hides were ripped from the carcasses. The hides were then scrapped of remaining flesh and the loaders began loading the hides onto the wagons. To Hiram and Joshua, it was a ghastly sight. They continued to watch for a short while.

"I can't watch any more of this Hiram."

"I guess the same sort of thing happens to the cattle when they hit the big processing houses. I never thought about it before, Joshua. But this is different. Knowing that these animals will be left to rot and the Indians up in the territory looked like they were starving, it makes me sick."

"You should try it from inside my skin."

"Well, we're stuck here for a while unless I can talk Stanford into outfitting us."

"We could always steal two horses." Joshua said jokingly.

"I don't think either one of us was cut out to be a horse thief. I'm gonna have another chat with Stanford. We're getting out of here."

Hiram didn't know exactly what he was going to say to Stanford, but he knew he would do whatever it took to move on. He had been thinking about Stanford's proposal. He rode to Stanford's coach deep in thought.

"Mr. Matthews. You watched our little operation. What do you think?"

"I think we need to talk, Mr. Stanford."

"All right, Mr. Matthews. Come on into the coach and we'll have a cup while we talk."

Stanford offered Hiram a seat and poured two cups of coffee. "What's on your mind, Mr. Matthews?"

"Stanford, I know that all this is business to you, but I can't abide it. I believe what you are doing is wrong. Senseless slaughter of these animals for just their hides just isn't right. Like I told you, I was a cattleman. I sent animals to the slaughter houses but the meat, the hides, almost every part of the animal is used for something. I don't understand how you can do this just to make money."

"Mr. Matthews, there's a part of me that agrees with you. If I could send these animals to market and have the whole animal used, I would do it. You tell me how to accomplish that and my profits skyrocket. I'm a capitalist. I make money. That's what I do."

"Then let's talk about changing how you make your money. I've been thinking about your proposition. I'm willing to talk about it with some provisions. Number one, you sell me two horses and provisions enough to get Joshua and me back to Waco. We leave immediately. Number two, you agree to make this your last big hunt. If we run cattle, we run cattle only. You said you have capital. I have some money from the sale of my ranch and cattle."

"Mr. Matthews, you're asking a lot. I want into the cattle business because I do believe it's the future, but it could take some time just to get even a small herd to market. I can't give up this market while I wait for another to develop. That's simply not good business."

"It may not take as long as you think. There are still a lot of wild longhorns and Castilian breed cattle roaming the open range in central and south Texas. The problem is rounding them up. That would require a number of wranglers, maybe ten, fifteen or more. You've already got that. I'm sure some of your men have worked cattle before. If they haven't, they can learn. I believe there are other small ranchers that would run their herd in with ours to get them to market. We would get a piece of that. We will need a base of operation and if things work out we will need land at some point. I can take care of that. There would be risk involved. We would be beyond the military frontier most of the time."

"I am willing to assume some risk. I would need more information about markets and prices."

"I don't know much about either. The war has changed everything else, so I assume the cattle markets are no different. My last herd sold out of Galveston at fourteen dollars a head. My guess is the war has driven the prices up. Armies have to eat. You figure out how to get 'em east and the price probably doubles on a head. Finding our best markets has to be your end of the business. I believe there is a good market supplying beef to the Union in Indian Territory. That brings me to my last provision. If we can establish a market in the territory, I want to be based there as our broker. I have a man in mind to manage the operation here in Texas once we're established in the Territory."

"You've thought this through in detail, Matthews. This hunt will be over in no more than a week. It will take at least a month to get these hides to market. I'll make a pact with you. I'll give you the two horses, a mule, and supplies. We can settle on those later. Go home and settle whatever business you have there. Meet me in Waco two months from today. Have everything on your end ready to go. I'll reach out to some contacts about the markets. If I can see the profit I need, you and I will be in the cattle business together."

"It's done then. We have a deal," Hiram said as he shook Stanford's hand.

"I insist that you give yourself another day or two to heal. My man can keep an eye on you and make sure that wound stays clean. Will you and Joshua take the evening meal with me and delay your departure until you're better?"

"We will."

Chapter Forty Two

"We'll be out of here in a couple of days, Joshua. I need a day or so to heal up some. Stanford agreed to give us two mounts, a mule and supplies."

"How in the devil did you talk him into that?"

"Well, I had to make a few concessions. It looks like I will be getting back into the cattle business. I'm afraid I sort of committed you too."

"That what you wanted?"

"I've been thinking about that a lot. We've been out here looking for Ethan for almost four months. I'm no closer now than when we left Waco. All we've done is run into trouble. I still think he's alive. I refuse to give up on that, but he could be anywhere from Mexico to the Territory - like everyone tried to tell me. Thinking I could find him in such a vast area with no real indication of where he could be probably is crazy."

"We can still head out to the Canadian."

"No, Joshua. I think all we would do wandering around out there is to get ourselves killed. I think it's time for me to accept the fact that Ethan may be lost to me. I've been thinking a lot about the folks living in the territory. They're in a bad way. There's a sadness in them, like there is in me. It's like they've lost something and can't get it back. Believe me, I know what that feels like. I can't say that I've ever seen people living in much worse conditions. I think about men like Holmes being in charge of helping those people, and I just can't imagine how that can be allowed."

"You don't hate the Comanche, do you?" Joshua asked.

"No, Joshua. I don't. I don't know that I've ever hated anyone, but I can see how it can happen to a man, how he can be driven to hate. I look at what's been done to the Comanche, the Kiowa, the Apache, all those people living up there – I can see how they've been driven to hate. I saw it in their faces and eyes. We've taken their lands; men like Stanford slaughtering the buffalo. We've stolen their lives. It's a shameful thing."

"It's been that way forever, Hiram. The Huaco, Kiowa, Apache – we were here when the Comanche came. The Spaniards, the Mexicans, the Comanche - they pushed most of us off of our native lands. Now the white man is pushing the Comanche out." He thought for a moment about Hiram's commitment to Stanford.

"You don't really like Stanford, do you?"

"I suppose he's likeable enough, that's not it. I just don't respect him that much. I don't agree with what he's doing. But I did get him to agree to stop killing buffalo if I go into business with him. So, like him or not, he's gonna be our partner."

There was a lull in the conversation. Both men were still considering all that had happened.

"You really givin' up searching, Hiram?"

"I've been thinking about that too, Joshua. I can't just forget Ethan and give up altogether. It seems inevitable that more and more of the Comanche are going to be forced into the territory. If that happens, who knows, maybe my boy will turn up some day. If I were to be up there at least I would be in a place to look."

Joshua was a bit confused. "Are you saying you want to go back to the Territory?" he asked.

"I want to visit Sarah's grave one more time, and I need to talk to Aaron. I made a deal with Stanford. If we can establish a market for cattle in the Territory, I told him I want to come back up here to broker the contracts if we can get them. And I'm not done with that Holmes fellow either."

Joshua did not respond right away. He was thinking about how far he might go if he were in his friend's shoes.

"You decide for sure that's what you want to do you may need an interpreter. I know a good one. Besides - and I hate to have to keep tellin' ya - "you ain't got good survival skills." They spoke in unison.

"Spoken like a true smart-ass." Hiram said with a grin.

Chapter Forty Three

By daylight of the third day Hiram and Joshua were ready to travel. Stanford had made good on his word and they were mounted and well provisioned. Stanford sat on his coach waiting for the men to depart.

"Mr. Stanford, I want to thank you again for all that you've done. We'll see you in Waco in two months."

"It's Amos. I think since we are going to be partners we should be on a first name basis. I look forward to seeing you in Waco. Joshua, I'm glad that you are staying on with us."

"That's something I wanted to clear up, Amos. Joshua will be a full partner with us or it's no deal."

"Capital. I'm glad to hear that, Hiram. We can work out all the details in Waco when we meet."

They shook hands again and Hiram and Joshua headed southeast toward Belknap.

They had ridden a short distance when Joshua spoke up. "You didn't mention me becoming a partner, Hiram. I didn't expect that at all. You know I can't pay for being a partner?"

"I don't expect you to pay. I owe you my life several times over and this is no gift. When we start rounding up cows, you'll earn your share. It's hard work daylight to dark. And it don't stop there. There's night riding once we start gathering a herd. Like I said, you'll earn it."

"You know I've never done anything like that?"

"I can teach you. You'll do."

"Then I guess we're partners. Yee Haw."

"Lesson number one. Don't ever do that with a bunch of seasoned cowboys around."

"Just tryin' to get in the spirit, Hiram!"

"I reckon we'll get in the spirit once we start rounding up a herd. I want to go back through Belknap. We can stay along the Brazos all the way to Waco when we're through there."

Seven days later they rode into Belknap. Lieutenant Helms was the O.D. and he saw them when they rode in.

"Mr. Matthews, I didn't expect to see you back here."

"I'm afraid that my search has come to an end for now, Lieutenant. We're on our way back to Waco. I had hoped to meet with Colonel Savage if possible."

"I am sure the Colonel will be anxious to meet with you. If you men will accompany me to his office I am sure he will meet with you right away."

The Colonel was delighted to see the two men alive and well. "Mr. Matthews, Joshua, you have been in my thoughts several times. Please tell me you were successful."

"Colonel, I'm afraid things didn't go so well." He shared the events that had taken place as the Colonel listened intently. "That Holmes fellow, he shouldn't be allowed to be in that position. That's part of why we came back through Belknap. I think you indicated that you have contacts. I would appreciate it if you could reach out to anyone you know to have him investigated. He's probably stealing from the government. I don't know that and can't prove it, but I'm willing to bet on it. He has no regard for the people up there. He is a man of low character."

"I will do what I can. I had no idea what kind of person he was. It's unfortunate that people of his lack of character can end up in such a position."

"Colonel, what became of Lieutenant Williams? He was seriously wounded."

"Williams recovered sufficiently to be sent where he could receive medical help. I'm afraid that he probably lost his arm. I've not received word of his fate at this point. He's a damn fine officer. I hated to lose him. Are you men planning on staying long?"

"I'm afraid not Colonel. The only reason we came back through Belknap was to speak with you about Holmes. I intend to see him removed from his position, one way or another."

"Well, rest assured that I will do everything I can to begin an investigation. I hope that you and Joshua will take the evening meal with me and my officers."

Hiram and Joshua left Belknap the following morning headed south east along the Brazos. They estimated that it would take about eight or ten days to reach Waco. There was no particular rush so Hiram had decided that they would take their time and simply enjoy the ride. They agreed that they would take the time to stop by the Paxton place to visit with John and Naomi.

Chapter Forty Four

Nathan and Leah Perelman moved from the San Antonio area to the area near the Brazos River fifty miles above Waco in 1858. Nathan worked in San Antonio for a number of years as a dry goods store owner and enjoyed some success, but he had never really been settled. He was a farmer at heart. His family had been farmers in Europe before they immigrated to Texas. He had grown up on a farm and he loved working the land. His family had come to San Antonio to be farmers. His mother and father had both died only a year after immigrating and had not yet been able to establish themselves. Nathan was only seventeen. He quickly learned that anti-Jewish sentiments were fairly strong in Texas. He changed his name from Perelman to Plemmons. He ended up going to work for a man who owned a dry goods store, and worked for the man for several years. When the owner decided to sell out, he had purchased the business. It was a decision brought on more from financial necessity than desire. He and Leah had been wed, and he knew he needed financial stability to provide for his new wife and the family that they planned. He had done well with the store until rumors went out that he was Jewish. Anti-Semitism was strong enough that his business began to suffer.

He and Leah wanted to start a family, but she was never able to bear children. It had been a huge disappointment for the couple. It had been coincidence that Nathan learned of a meeting arranged with a band of Comanches to discuss trade for release of white hostages being held. He had told Leah of the meeting and they decided to go out of curiosity.

The Comanche brought women and children to the meeting. One shy little boy had caught their attention. When it became apparent that no one was present to claim the boy, they quickly decided that they would take him. The boy had obviously been harshly treated and had evidence on his body that he had been tortured. His tongue had been mutilated and most of the time he refused to attempt to speak. They took the boy and made him their son. They named him Joseph, after Leah's father. He was fearful and given to fits of fright, especially at night. He had been affected mentally by the torture and seemed to have no recollection of his past beyond the time of his abduction. Leah and Nathan had been patient and worked with the boy, always assuring him that he was safe and loved. He had begun to respond to their tender care and after more than a year he had settled into life with his new family, and the fearfulness had begun to pass.

Nathan's business had dropped off and when he had found that he could still claim land in Texas under the Homestead Act, he and Leah had discussed selling the business and finding some land on which they could raise cotton. He had figured out a budget that would allow them to use their savings and the money from the sale of the business to purchase the goods they would need to start. He had figured that after expenditures they could survive financially for at least a year or more. They had picked the area and settled on one hundred and sixty acres provided by the state of Texas.

It had been hard work establishing a farm. Fields had to be cleared, a house had to be built, and barns and livestock corrals had to be made. Nathan and Leah had never been happier. By the end of their first year they had a livable home and Nathan had cleared enough area to produce a good crop of cotton. Leah had planted a small garden and raised enough vegetables to supply their needs many months of the year. Young Joseph had taken to life on the farm. Even at his young age he helped Leah with the garden and had shown a knack for working with the farm animals. He could milk a cow and he tended the chickens and pigs. He could speak a bit, but refused to most of the time. They always figured it was because he was self-conscious about how he sounded. It made no difference to Nathan and Leah. They loved the boy as their own, and he had responded to the love that they had shown him. Except for the speech and the occasional fearfulness, he had become a fairly normal little boy.

They had worked hard as a family unit. As Joseph had grown he was able to help Nathan more and more with the clearing and plowing and harvesting. Once the war started, Nathan had found that he could sell large quantities of potatoes in Waco. He had met a businessman lawyer there named Zebediah Granger and he was willing to buy everything that Nathan could produce. They had begun producing potatoes on almost half of the cleared land. It was a much easier crop to plant and harvest. The cotton crop required that Nathan find slave owners nearby who would allow him to use their slaves during the harvest. It was costly and Nathan hated the idea of slavery.

Joseph was becoming an excellent farmer and could handle a plow and team better than Nathan. He too had apparently learned to love working the land. They had never experienced a severe drought year and had done well selling the large crops of potatoes and cotton. Nathan and Leah had begun talking about how they could expand their farm. They had become a happy, prospering family.

Chapter Forty Five

Hiram and Joshua had continued their journey home at a casual pace. They had actually found several farms along the Brazos and had visited briefly with a couple of families. They had spent time talking and had come to know one another even better. They both had actually begun to look forward to their new venture. On the sixth day out from Belknap, Hiram's mount came up lame.

"I don't think this mare can even carry our packs. She's limping pretty badly. I think she can walk, but there's no way she's carrying any load. Looks like I'm walking again."

"I figure we got four hours of daylight left, Hiram. Why don't we make camp? I'll ride ahead a way and see if there may be another farm or ranch, anything."

"I suppose a little more rest won't hurt anything. It may do the mare good too."

After they had made camp Joshua rode ahead. Luck was with them again. About two miles out he spotted a small farm house surrounded by well cultivated fields. He decided not to go in alone and turned back to camp.

"Found a farm about two miles out, Hiram. Looks like a nice place. I didn't go in. You think that mare can walk two miles?"

"I guess we'll find out tomorrow."

Fate was about to intervene in Hiram Matthew's life.

The next morning the mare was still limping but she was able to make the two miles. Both men had walked the entire distance. As they approached the farm they saw a young man working the far end of one of the fields. They led their mounts toward the barn where there was a hitch rail. As they were tying their mounts a man exited the barn. He was a bit startled when he looked up and saw strangers.

"Hello," he said. "Can I help you fellows?"

"Sorry we startled you. My mare came up lame a ways back. My friend here saw your farm and we walked in this morning."

"I'm Nathan Plemmons," he said as he stuck out his hand.

"Hiram Matthews. This is my friend Joshua." Hiram replied.

"You said your horse is injured?"

"Well, I honestly don't know what's wrong with her. There aren't any stones and her shoes are okay."

"Unfortunately I'm not that good with animals," said Plemmons.

"Do you have a mount that you would sell me?"

"Unfortunately, I really don't. We have our mules, but I can't let one of those go."

"Are there other farms or ranches close by?"

Plemmons didn't answer right away. "You fellows just passing through?"

"Well, we're bound for Waco. Have to meet a friend of mine. He's a lawyer there."

"I know a few folks in Waco. What would be your friend's name?"

"Zeb. Zeb Granger."

"I'll just be darned," Plemmons replied. "Judge Granger operates several enterprises there. He buys potatoes and cotton from us. Been doing business with him for a few years. He's a good man."

"Yes, sir. He has been my friend for many years. Did you say Judge Granger?"

"Well it is a small world. And yes sir, I called him Judge Granger. You asked about another farm. There is another place about two, three miles south. They are a larger operation than we are. They may have horses."

"Then one of us has to go, Joshua. I think it has to be me. Mr. Plemmons, will it be all right if my friend stays here?"

"Oh, sure. That will be fine. If you stay to the river you can't miss the place. Like I said they are a bigger operation. They raise a lot of cotton."

"I should be back before dark. We can be on our way if I can buy another mount."

"There's no need to rush off. If you're back in time, you and your friend are welcome to take supper with me and my family.

"Then I'll be on my way."

Hiram made the ride in a short while. On the way he thought how fortunate it was that he had grabbed his saddle bags the day the raiding party had hit them. They contained his money, the toy pistol, and the broach.

The owners of the farm did in fact have horses and after a bit of bargaining, he had purchased a fine mare. He was soon on his way back to the Plemmons farm. He arrived well before supper time and Plemmons invited him and Joshua in for coffee and introduced them to Leah.

"I didn't think you would be back this soon. I would introduce you to my son, but he's actually still working one of our potato fields. He'll be coming in soon. He's a good kid. He's probably only ten or twelve, but he can handle a team better than me."

"You're not sure how old your son is?" Hiram asked.

"Oh, I'm sorry, Mr. Matthews. That must have been confusing. Leah and I adopted Joseph. We don't know anything about his background. We come from San Antonio. A number of years back there was a band of Comanches that had arranged a trade to release some hostages. We went to see what that was all about and when it became clear that Joseph had no one to claim him, we decided to adopt him. You wouldn't believe the difference in him now versus then. He had been tortured by his captors. They cut out part of his tongue. He doesn't speak much. We think it's that he is self-conscious about how he sounds.

Honestly, he's a bit slow. Probably a result of the trauma he suffered at the hands of his captors. But he's a good kid. Really a hard worker and loves working the land. We couldn't love him more if he were our own flesh and blood. He's been a Godsend."

Hiram's mind was racing but he said nothing. He looked at Joshua and by the look of astonishment he saw that he was thinking the same thing. He still had not spoken.

"Mr. Matthews, are you all right? You look like you just saw a ghost. I hope being frank about how Joseph was treated didn't upset you."

Hiram fought to regain his composure.

"No. Everything is fine," he said weakly.

"Sometimes I speak before I think. Some folks are squeamish about that sort of thing. I guess we're just used to how things are. And I certainly didn't mean to offend you either, Joshua."

Joshua simply shook his head.

"I look forward to meeting your son. I believe Joshua and I need to tend our animals and clean up before supper."

"Of course," said Leah. "Where are my manners? I'll fetch you a cloth and you can clean up out at the well."

Hiram and Joshua headed for the barn. Hiram was almost weak in the knees.

"My God, Joshua. Their son could be my Ethan."

"Whoa, partner. That's a big leap. One thing at a time. He said they adopted their boy down in San Antonio. You were always sure that your boy was taken north. Don't get all worked up over something that just ain't likely."

Hiram shook his head. "You're right Joshua. I've been wishing for so long. Now I'm jumping at anything."

"Let's just get cleaned up and go on back to the house. These folks are fine people and it wouldn't be good to say something and get them all upset over nothing."

"You're right, Joshua." Hiram replied.

Leah had prepared a fine meal and they all set waiting for young Joseph to finish washing up. Hiram sat with his back to the door. Presently Joseph came in, hungry and ready to eat.

"Ah. There you are Joseph," Leah said cheerily. "We have company tonight."

Hiram rose and turned to meet the young man. He almost jumped out of his skin. It was as if he were looking at himself when he was the same age. The blood drained from his face and he felt almost as if he would faint.

"Mr. Matthews this is our son Joseph," Leah said happily. She looked at Hiram and was almost startled. "Mr. Matthews are you all right?" she said.

Nathan also noticed the look on Hiram's face. "You look like you saw the ghost again, Mr. Matthews. You're absolutely pale. Are you coming down with something?"

Hiram needed to get out of the room. "I'm not feeling well. I think I'll go lay down in the barn for a while. I'm sorry Mrs. Plemmons."

"Don't you think anything about it. You are welcome to lay down in our room." she said.

"That's awfully nice of you, but the barn will be fine. Our bedrolls are already laid out."

"You go right ahead. I'll bring supper out to you after a bit. Maybe you just need some rest."

Joshua was unsure what to do. "You need me to walk out with you Hiram?"

"No, Joshua. You eat dinner with these good folks. I'll be fine." He stole another look at Joseph. The boy stared straight back and gave no indication that he recognized Hiram. Neither Nathan nor Leah had seemed to notice the resemblance between Hiram and Joseph. Hiram excused himself and headed to the barn. Joshua finished the fine meal prepared by Leah and excused himself.

"If it's not too rude I'd like to go check on Hiram."

"Absolutely not. You go check on your friend and I'll be out with some food later," said Leah.

He found Hiram sitting on a bucket in the barn with his head in his hands. It almost looked like he was praying.

"You okay Hiram?"

"No. No, I'm not okay. It's him Joshua. It's Ethan."

"You sure?"

"My God. Yes, I'm sure. If you had known me when I was that age, you wouldn't even need to ask."

Joshua thought about what his friend must be going through. "The boy gave no indication that he knew you. He would have reacted if he had. You're absolutely sure it's him?"

"I'm as certain of it as I am certain of who I am."

"So what you gonna do?"

"I don't know. I'm sure that Ethan didn't know me. He certainly didn't show it if he did. I keep hanging around and he starts remembering things, what happens then? These folks are his family now. If I say anything it could just confuse him. Not to mention what it might do to Nathan and Leah. You warned me, Joshua. Everything in me wants to go back in there and tell them everything. They look at both of us together very long they'll know it's the truth. But what will it do to them all?"

"It's not for me to tell you what to do. You want my opinion?"

"No."

"Okay. Here's what I think."

"I said no."

"Yeah. But your heart wasn't in it. Suppose you tell him and the Plemmons. He still don't know you. You show him the toy and the broach. Maybe he remembers. He may remember you, but he still don't know you. You want him to ride off to Waco with you? That ain't gonna happen. You said it. These folks are his family now. Tell them now, it just messes things up."

"My head agrees with you. But I lost him once. How can I lose him again?"

"Hell, Hiram. He ain't lost. You know exactly where he is and where he's gonna be. Maybe you come back this way from time to time to visit these folks. Maybe you come back some day when he's grown and tell him the truth."

Hiram sat silent for a long while deep in thought. He finally spoke. "Joshua, you're right. I think it would be cruel to let these folks know who I am. Ethan can't know. Not right now. Like you said, maybe some day when he's a man. But I have to tell you, Joshua, this hurts like crazy."

Leah had prepared a plate for Hiram and she called to the men from outside the barn door. "Is it okay if I bring Mr. Mathews in a plate?"

"Please. I'm actually feeling better."

Leah entered and handed Hiram the plate. "I'd feel better if you weren't eating in a barn, Mr. Matthews."

"No, that's fine. I really do feel better now. Joshua and I were just talking. We really need to get on to Waco. We will be leaving early in the morning and I think I'll turn in after I eat. I still may be coming down with something. May be best I don't expose you folks any more than necessary. I'm sorry I won't get to properly meet Joseph. Who knows, maybe we'll be back this way. You are fine folks and I appreciate the hospitality that you've shown us."

"Well, you're always welcome here, Mr. Matthews. I'll let Nathan know. He will likely be up before daybreak and will want to say goodbye."

The two men saddled up the next morning before daybreak. Nathan came to the barn to bid them farewell. "What do you want to do with the injured horse Mr. Matthews?" Nathan asked.

"She's of no good to us, Mr. Plemmons. You keep her and see if she heals up if you like. If she doesn't recover, will you put her down for me?" Plemmons agreed and after good byes, they were again on their way to Waco.

"I think this may be the hardest thing I've ever done, Joshua."

"Well, we both know it's the right thing."

"Yeah, I know. But it don't help much."

Chapter Forty Six

The two men continued their ride to Waco. They stopped at the Paxton's and visited with John and Naomi for a day. They were now nearing Waco.

"I figure we're no more than two miles from my place, Hiram. It's just right down the river a way."

"You want to drop off at your place that's fine. I can ride on in and take care of business with Zeb. We can spend the night at your place if that's all right."

Joshua had agreed and Hiram rode into Waco alone. As he rode to Zeb's office he was being carefully watched. He would soon clash with a man he had never expected to see again.

Zeb Granger had fully expected to never see Hiram Matthews again. He had thought of Hiram on several occasions, wondering what had befallen him in his search; wondering if he were still alive. But he had also been a busy man. The citizens of Waco had pressed Zeb to become a judge. There was a need for a good court system in the emerging town. Zeb had finally agreed with the stipulation that it not interfere with his business interests. He had changed the sign on his office door to read "Judge Zebediah Granger". Most of his time as a judge was spent dealing with civil disputes and minor criminal infractions, but he soon found that he actually loved the job.

He heard the office door open and looked up. He jumped to his feet and almost ran to the man entering.

"By god, Hiram," he said as he grabbed him in a bear hug. He pushed back and held Hiram by his shoulders. "I've thought of you often, but I honestly thought I would likely never see you again."

"It's good to see you again Judge Granger. Really good."

Zeb released his grip on his friend. "I guess you read what was on the door. The good citizens of Waco insisted on it. Impressive, huh? I'm guessing that you're back here because of something awfully important." He pointed to two calf skin covered wing back chairs made by a local craftsman. "Have a seat. You'll like the chairs. Had 'em made just the way I wanted them. I want to hear everything that has happened. Start from the beginning and don't leave anything out. And please tell me you were successful."

Hiram related the full story to Zeb. As requested he gave him the long version including his run in with Mallory and the two raiding parties. He had not yet included the best part.

"So I take it you were unsuccessful in finding your son."

"I guess that's the final part of my story, Zeb."

"Go on, go on."

Hiram told of their trip home along the Brazos to Waco and the mind boggling events that had taken place at the Plemmons.

"By god, Hiram. Your son has been living that close all this time. I suppose that's a cruel turn of fate. Must have been hard for you. I'd like to meet the boy."

"Zeb, he's not with us. We left him with his adopted family."

Hiram went on to relate how he had come to his decision. "I decided that it would be even more cruel for Ethan to know. The Plemmons are as nice a family as you'll ever meet. They love Ethan as much as anyone could. We left hastily so that there was little if any chance of him knowing who I am. I tell you Zeb, it near ripped out my heart, but I knew it was the right thing to do. It was Joshua convinced me. He's become a good friend."

"I'm glad you took my advice and took him along. There's little doubt that you would be dead if he hadn't been with you."

"He's saved my life at least twice."

"I want to meet him, Hiram."

"You will Zeb. We're staying the night in his hut up river. And I guess that brings me to the real reason we came back to Waco. I'm going back into the cattle business. The Stanford fellow I told you about is going to be my partner. Joshua will be an equal third party. I want you to draw up papers. They will need to spell out the details. I'll set back down with you tomorrow and we can discuss it. At some point we will need to acquire land as a base of operation and I'll need your help with that."

"Well, it's strange that you come back here wanting to go back into the cattle business. I have some news for you concerning just that. Truthfully, I never expected to have the opportunity to tell you. After you left, Will Hardison came by to see me. We discussed you selling him the ranch. He wanted it badly, but couldn't understand why you had decided to sell it to him. I told him the whole story. He felt bad about it all afterward. He did the damnedest thing I've ever heard. He asked me to put a hold on finishing the transaction for six months. Refused to make the deposit of the money. He felt like he was taking advantage of you. We talked to Scoggins and he agreed that without the funds being deposited there was no sale. The ranch still belongs to you. Will Hardison has got to be the most honest man I've ever known, that is other than you my friend."

Hiram sat for a moment while the shocking story sunk in. "I hardly see how that's right, Zeb. I made a deal with Will. Gave him my word and we shook on it."

"I'm willing to wager he won't have this any other way. If he still wants more land I'll help him find it. I told him that. Think about it. If you're going to start running cattle again, maybe Will would be interested in being a part of that in some way. It could turn out to be a good deal for both of you."

"I'll think on it. I'd like to talk to Will first. "What about Aaron, Jake, and Hank?"

"Will and I agreed to pay Jake and Hank to keep things going at the ranch. I've not spoken to them. I assume Aaron made it back to the ranch. You'll have to reimburse Will for their pay. If you need money, I'll make you a personal loan."

"I'm fine. That won't be necessary. There is one more thing. I want you to draw me up a will. I want to name Joseph Plemmons as my heir and I want to make sure there's something for Joshua. If everything goes well, I'd like to send a little money the Plemmons' way from time to time. We can work all that out tomorrow too."

"Then we'll handle all of this tomorrow. Maybe we can all take supper together tomorrow evening."

"That will be fine, but not where we went before."

"Can't say I blame you there," Zeb laughed. "I'll ask Julia Smith if she can prepare us something special."

Hiram and Zeb shook hands and Hiram stopped in the door way. "I think things have turned out okay, Zeb. It's gonna be all right."

He closed the door and turned to walk back to his mount.

"Hello, Cowboy."

The voice startled Hiram. He turned and was looking down the barrel of a big bore Sharp's rifle. The man holding it was Kevin Mallory and he stood no more than a dozen feet away. He was thinner and stood with a stoop, but it was him.

"Yeah. You know who I am all right." Mallory was gloating and savoring the moment he had sought for months. "You just knew I was dead didn't ya. Hadn't of been for a couple of buffalo hunters I would have been. Your bad luck Cowboy. You should have shot me like I begged ya' to. You know what it's like to beg to die? Took a lot of asking questions to find out all about you. Something told me you'd be back here some day. I'm a patient man Cowboy. And now I'm gonna blow your damned head off.

Then I'm gonna find that Indian and give him a slice for every time my gut feels like it's still got that arrow in it."

Hiram thought quickly. If he didn't find a way out of his current mess, he didn't want Mallory going after Joshua. "He's dead. Got killed in a scrape with Comanches."

"You're lying' Cowboy."

"Nope. He's dead all right." Hiram's brain was buzzing trying to find a way to get Mallory distracted. "But if you'd care to look over your left shoulder you'll see my friend. You strung him up in that oak tree with me. He's got his rifle on you, and you shoot me, he shoots you." Hiram lied.

"Don't matter. I reckon the pleasure of seeing your head explode will do. The Indian don't really matter either." Mallory retorted. But the play worked. He stole just a small glance over his shoulder. When he looked away for that split second, Hiram dived to his right and reached for the Army pistol that hung on his left side. Mallory was a bit too slow to react. The big rifle erupted and his shot went wild. The huge bullet traveled a hundred feet down the street and struck a bystander dead. Mallory reached for another round. Hiram sprang to his feet and rushed him. Mallory looked back up just as the barrel of the big revolver came crashing to the side of his head. He slumped to his knees and keeled over onto his side.

Zeb heard the report of the big rifle and came rushing from his office. He saw Hiram standing over the man with his pistol drawn.

"By god. What the hell happened here?"

"Meet Mr. Kevin Mallory," Hiram said as he rolled Mallory over with his boot. "It was his buffalo gun you heard."

"That's the fellow you had the run in with. You told me he was killed by your friend."

"Appears he didn't die from his wounds. I can't believe he survived."

A small crowd had begun to gather. One of the men standing in the crowd spoke up.

"I seen it all Judge. That feller layin in the street fired that big bufflo' gun at this here feller. He ain't much of a shot I guess. Missed this feller, but he killed Elmer Giddings dead as a hammer. That's him that crowd's gathered around down the street."

"Will someone please fetch the sheriff?" Zeb asked.

The same man spoke up. "I'll get him for ya', Judge."

"By god, Hiram. I believe you've got more lives than a cat."

"Danged lucky Mallory was slow again. Probably drunk. I'll just keep him covered 'till the sheriff gets here. Hopefully, this is the last time I'll ever have to deal with him."

"Oh, you can rest assured. He's going to swing. He killed one of our citizens. I'll give him a speedy trial followed by a first class hanging. I don't believe we've ever had a hanging in Waco."

"What about the man he killed?"

"Truth is Hiram, he's a drunk and a worthless scoundrel. I guess if Mallory had to kill someone, Elmer would be the least unfortunate choice. Still a damned senseless thing."

"A man like Mallory doesn't care. His kind live on whiskey and violence."

After the sheriff had taken Mallory away, Hiram said goodbye to Zeb again and headed out to join Joshua for the evening. He knew he had quite a story to tell over supper.

Chapter Forty Seven

Zeb, Joshua, and Hiram spent several hours the next day working out the terms of the partnership and in getting a new will written. That evening they visited Julia Smith as planned. She had closed early and prepared a special meal just for the Judge and his friends.

The following morning they started back to the ranch and on the following day they rode in. The men were mending corral and saw them when they rode up. Hiram and Joshua reined their horses in at the corral.

"Howdy fellas." said Hiram.

"I'll be danged. I can't believe it's you boss. I doubted we would ever see you again," Jake said through a big grin.

"By danged," said Hank.

Aaron walked to Hiram's mount and stuck out a hand. "You boys lost? Good to see you again Hiram." He stuck out his hand to Joshua. "Damn glad to see you too Joshua. I see you two managed to keep your scalps."

"You look mended, Aaron. Good to see you men," Hiram said.

Hank and Jake had come over to shake Hiram's hand. Neither man offered a hand to Joshua. Hiram took note.

"I take it you haven't found Ethan," said Aaron.

"I've some things to tell you fellows. It includes news of my son. You boys still drink coffee?"

"Not when you work for Aaron Russell," Jake said laughingly.

"Hard boss is he?" Hiram asked.

"Naw, he's just partial to using any daylight there might be," joked Hank.

"Well, I still drink coffee. You want to go up to the house or the bunk house," Aaron asked.

"You know, I think I'd like to set at my kitchen table again fellows. Let's all go up and put a pot on. I'll tell you all the whole story."

"We'll take care of the horses and we'll be along in a few minutes." Aaron offered.

The coffee was made and Hiram began to relate the events that had passed. The three men sat captivated by the story of all that had happened. It took a while for Hiram to tell it all. He had left out the part about the agreement with Amos Stanford, the ranch, and his intention of resuming the operation.

"All that searching and your boy living not more than three or four days ride away all that time," Aaron said as he shook his head. "Life don't make much sense sometimes."

"I can definitely agree with that, Aaron. But I think I'm content knowing where Ethan is and that he's happy. I couldn't ask for more. That I found him at all is nothing short of a bona fide miracle. God willing, the day will come when I can tell him everything."

"I sure hope so, Boss. You gave up the ranch and everything else to find him," Hank chimed in.

"Boys, that's the other thing we need to talk about. It seems Will Hardison doesn't want to buy the ranch. There's a story behind it all, but all you need to know is the ranch is still mine if I want it. I've got to talk to Will about it all, but I'm inclined to take Will's offer. I told you about the man Stanford. What I didn't tell you is that I made a deal with him to go back into the cattle business with him. We intend to raise a big herd quickly. That's my job. Finding the best markets will be Stanford's job. My intent is to start rounding up a herd right away. The problem is that we will probably have to go out beyond the protected frontier to do it. There's risk involved there. Comanches,

Mexicans, gun runners, thieves, you name it. We'll have to go west and south. Round up small herds and drive them back here. We keep that up till we have the herd we need for our first drive. It will take wranglers for all this and Stanford has ample men available. It won't be easy, but I believe we can do it.

There's one more thing. Joshua I hope you won't mind my frankness here. Hank, Jake - You expressed a concern once about working with an Indian. Said you wouldn't do it. You need to know – you'll be working for me and Joshua. He's a full partner in this thing. If you can't do it that will be your decision, but there won't be a place for you here if that's your decision. Aaron, once we get this thing going there could be times when Joshua and I need to be gone. Maybe months at a time. I'll need you running things on this end during those times. I'll make sure all your wages fit the job we have to do. I guess that's the long and short of it fellows."

The men thought about it for a few minutes.

"Boss when you brought Joshua here the first time it wasn't under the best situation. You say he's your partner and friend now, that's good enough for me. I'm in." Jake said with resolve and stuck out his hand to Joshua.

Hank was silent for a moment as he mulled over what Hiram had said. At length he spoke up. "I'm sorry but I reckon I'll have to be moving on, Boss. It ain't about working with you, Joshua. I just don't want to get my scalp lifted. I ain't no Indian fighter. I'm just not willing to take the chance. No hard feelings, Joshua, Boss. Like Jake said, you're okay by the boss, you're okay by me," He stuck out his hand to Joshua.

"You change your mind, Hank, let me know. Aaron you okay on this?"

"I'm in all the way Hiram."

"Then I guess that's it. We'll work out the details as we go. Now, if you fellows will excuse me there's something I need to do."

Hiram left the house and picked up his saddlebags. He walked slowly out to the oak tree where Sarah lay. He sat down next to her marker and ran his finger around the lettering that he had carved when he had laid her to rest. At length he began to speak.

"I ho...." Hiram's voice choked. The weight of all that had happened - all the hope, all the disappointments, all the hurt and sorrow, and now the happiness of finding his son - finally came crashing down on Hiram. He choked back the tears. "I hope you can hear me, Sarah. In my heart I believe you can." He paused for a while. "I found him Sarah. I found Ethan. The Indians that took him sold him to a family down in San Antonio. Their name is Plemmons. They call him Joseph. He looks like me, but he's still got your eyes. The Plemmons love him like their own. They're really fine people. They're farmers. He already works a team of mules like a grown ma...." He choked back the tears again. "I couldn't bring him here. Not yet. Some day when I think he's ready I'll tell him about you Sarah and how much you loved him. Maybe he'll come back here with me when it's time." He paused again for a long while. "I'll make sure that he never wants for anything. I'm so sorry I didn't do this for you when you were still with me." The tears came again.

He took his knife and began to dig a small hole at the base of Sarah's marker. He reached into his saddle bags and withdrew a piece of tattered cloth. He removed the small toy pistol and the broach and placed them in the hole. He moved the earth back into place and patted it with his hand. He sat silently for a great while longer. At sundown he rose and stood over Sarah's grave. "You rest now," he said softly. He turned and walked toward the house. Hiram Matthews was finally at peace.

CPSIA information can be obtained
at www.ICGtesting.com
Printed in the USA
LVHW101125130123
737055LV00018B/156